ELEANOR MERRY

Dark Valentine Holiday Horror Collection: A Flash Fiction Anthology

First published by EMerry Publishing 2020

This novel is entirely a work of fiction. The names, characters and incidents portrayed in it are the work of the author's imagination. Any resemblance to actual persons, living or dead, events or localities is entirely coincidental.

Designations used by companies to distinguish their products are often claimed as trademarks. All brand names and product names used in this book and on its cover are trade names, service marks, trademarks and registered trademarks of their respective owners. The publishers and the book are not associated with any product or vendor mentioned in this book. None of the companies referenced within the book have endorsed the book.

First edition

ISBN: 978-1-9992128-7-2

Editing by Alexander Shedd
Cover art by Brian Scutt

This book was professionally typeset on Reedsy.
Find out more at reedsy.com

This book is dedicated to one of the authors of this collection, Robert Chester Ferguson Jr., who passed away in 2010. A Navy Seal Wolf, Robert "Chett" dreamed of being an author, and we thank his daughter, Danielle, for sharing his work with us.
May his words live on forever.

Contents

Foreword

How will you celebrate the holidays?

Dark Valentine is a collection of 99 flash fiction and drabble stories that showcase the dark and depraved side of this holiday of love.

Blood and guts.

Tears and sorrow.

Revenge and justice.

Sex and lust.

This is our Dark Valentine, and it is not for the faint of heart.

Dark Valentine is book 2 in the holiday horror collection.

With stories from over thirty authors including Eleanor Merry, Cassandra Angler, Angela Glover, M. Ennenbach, P.J. Blakey-Novis, Sea Caummisar, Galina Trefil, DJ Elton, N.M. Brown, Scott Deegan, Alanna Robertson-Webb, Terry Miller, Trisha McKee, Dawn DeBraal, Archit Joshi, Galina Trefil, Andrew Kurtz, Jason Myers, Andra Dill, Matthew A. Clarke, Alexander Shedd, Sheila Shedd, Ximena Escobar, Nerisha Kemraj, Zoey Xolton, Kevin J. Kennedy, Chris Miller, Lea Vida Del Moro, Wendy Cheairs, Amber M. Simpson, James Pyles, Robert Chester Ferguson Jr, Danielle Sandidge, Joel R. Hunt, Lance Dale, Nicole Henning, Nico Bell, Joshua E. Borgmann, Natasha Sinclair, Daileas Duclo, David Simms, Andrea Allison, Chris Bannor, Aaron Channel, Aindrila Roy and Zachary C. Collier.

Dark Valentine's by Scott Deegan

In a time of love and lust
  Hidden beneath ash and dust
  The heart tells only lies
  Crawling over broken dreams
  Finding only blood and screams
  Here's where all desire dies
  Trapped in a web of endless pain
  Relationships made in vain
  The truth shines bright and bold
  From burning deep in lustful nights
  To cutting words in mindless fights
  The flames dying in the cold
  Here you'll find the dark verses
  Whispered of eternal curses
  To lovers gone astray
  Stories of revenge served black
  Of words you can't take back
  On this, Dark Valentine's Day!

Be Mine by Jason Myers

Last year you agreed. Last year you said you would always be my Valentine. Well, here we are in the second week of February and you're still with him. A promise is a promise. And I am coming to collect.

I bet you didn't think I could track you down. I bet you didn't think I could find your new apartment in such a big city. I bet you think you were *so* clever changing your name and phone number. Do you think a little piece of paper that says "Protection Order" can really stop us from being together? The heart wants what the heart wants. And mine wants yours.

How foolish of the concierge at your building to let me in. Some bullshit story about *me being your brother* and *I'm here to visit* is all it took? I think you would need to inquire about getting some money back on your rent agreement if that is the "added security" that you pay for. Not that it will matter anymore.

Wrong place, wrong time. I suppose I should've expected him to be there waiting for you, it being Valentine's Day and all. All the planning, all the preparation and that little variable never came to mind.

Simple fix.

I won't hurt your image of him. I won't tell you what he cried out as he begged me stop. I won't let you know how he promised that you and him never touched until way after the divorce papers were signed. I'm your white knight, not him. Remember when you called me that?

If I had more time I suppose I could go through this 8th floor apartment and remove all the pictures and reminders of him. If I had more time I could cook up some spare ribs and potatoes. Those were always your favorites. If

I had more time I would light the candles that he already has out and put on some slow elevator music. However, as luck would have it, time is not a luxury even in this luxury apartment. I have so much prepping to do before you come home. I have to line the floors with plastic. The couches, the table, the chairs. Yes, time is really flying by waiting for you to come home. Although our real home is still 500 miles west of here.

They say it's hard to find everything you need in one place but the hardware store really is the best bang for your buck. Duct tape, rope, ball peen hammer, mop? Check. Hydrofluoric acid was the only odd item needed but thanks to the internet, it wasn't an issue. Time to get ready for your homecoming. Fuses pulled, pitch black, waiting behind the island in the kitchen. Come home to me. Come home and be mine forever. I'll be waiting for the doorknob to turn. I'll be waiting for life to suddenly make sense again.

Be my Valentine, or be no one's.

Perfect by Cassandra Angler

Erica stood looking at herself in her full length mirror. She had a date for Valentine's Day for the first time in years and wanted it to be perfect. She bought a new bra and panty set that she wore now as she surveyed her body. She frowned at the small pouch at the bottom of her belly that hung over the front of her panties. Turning, she huffed at the love handles. Not hidden well enough for her liking.

"He's never going to want me like this," she muttered to herself.

Walking into the kitchen, Erica grabbed the meat cleaver from its place on the wall and returned to the mirror. She took a deep breath and grabbed the excess skin on her stomach.

"One. Two. Three."

On three, Erica slid the knife along her stomach. It burned as the skin detached from her body and dropped to the floor. She looked down at the little blob of fat and kicked it across the floor. Looking at herself now, her stomach now flat, Erica smiled. She continued to cut, first the love handles she hated so much and then the skin on her underarms that hung in a way she felt unflattering.

She twirled in the mirror, blood splattering in a perfect circle around her. The doorbell rang and she clapped excitedly. She wrapped her robe around herself and answered the door.

Fredrick's eager smile fell into a concerned frown as he saw Erica's legs covered in blood.

"Are you okay?" he asked, voice trembling.

"Never better," Erica said cheerily. "Come on inside, have a seat."

She sat him on the couch and stood in front of him, waving her hips back and forth. She unknotted her robe and let it fall to the floor, sticky and caked with blood. Fredrick screamed and jumped up from the couch.

"I know it's a little forward," Erica said, "but I thought you'd be happy."

"What did you do?!" he cried in horror.

"Just a little modifying. Don't you like it?"

Fredrick backed up, arms up in surrender. He fell backwards, slipping on something wet and slippery. Looking down, he saw the small ball of belly flesh Erica had cut from herself. He jumped up, and ran out of the house screaming, not bothering to close the door behind him.

Erica stood in the doorway, her hands on her hips as she watched him pull away. Returning to the mirror, meat cleaver in hand, she began to cry.

"It's my face, isn't it?" she asked her reflection.

With a sigh, she pulled out one of her cheeks and slid the blade through the skin.

Just A Group of Nice Guys by Scott Deegan

"My name is John and I'm a nice guy," the man in the bow tie and fedora said.

"Hi, John," a chorus of voices replied.

"I have a friend who only dates guy that are wrong for her. She's always getting her heart broken and then comes crawling back to me wanting to know why she can't find a decent guy. Well hello, m'lady, I'm right here and always have been." John paused as the rest of the group responded with sounds confirming this scenario.

"I have been her friend and tried to wait as she came to her senses, but a guy can only keep quiet so long. I told her how I felt about her and how well I would treat her if she was mine, but she says we're just friends. God, how I hate that saying. So I've waited time and again while she whores herself out to every piece of shit fuck-boy that looks like the latest pop sensation and the same thing happens. Wham, bam, thank ya ma'am! I couldn't sit idly by and watch her continue to act like a cheap slut. I had to step in for her own good, I had to save her. So, last weekend I waited for her to return home from going down on the flavor of the week. As she was trying to get her drunk whore ass in the door, I snuck up and chloroformed her. She's chained in my basement until she can learn to love me. I believe I actually have a shot with this one, unlike the one before her who continued to resist loving me and had to be put down for her own good. I want to thank Mike and Dr. Steve for helping dispose of the body, you guys are great. Thank you for letting me share my story." John returned to his seat.

"Thank you, John," the chorus came again.

"I hope her tits burn off in hell!" someone yelled from the back.

"Okay, settle down. Who else would like to share?" Dr. Steve asked.

Plant by Chris Miller

I clutch the flowers tightly as I near the corner, the one just before her apartment. She'd posted on Facebook how much she likes plants. Funny, the way she puts things sometimes. One of many reasons I'm here now. The way she talks. Her terminology.

If I have any secret admirers out there this Valentine's Day, remember: I LOVE PLANTS!

Flowers, of course. That's what she meant. But it's all part of her charm. Her refusal to conform, all the way down to her choice of words. As beautiful as she is.

I'm thinking of what I might say. How to phrase it. What's a cute way of telling a woman how you feel about her that won't come off as either cheesy or creepy? I know I'm taking a risk showing up to her apartment unannounced. So far, our exchanges at work have been little more than polite pleasantries. They always start with a nod and a smile, more forced than I'd like, but she doesn't really know me yet. After the smile and nod, maybe a "Good morning!" or a "How's your day going?"

I force my feet forward so I don't lose my nerve. I round the corner, and I'm there. Her place. Her apartment. There's a lovely welcome mat in front—cats sprawled over a couch—and a heart-shaped wreath hanging on the open front door.

The door is open. My breath seizes. Is she on her way out? Worse, is she headed out on a date? It's February 14th, after all.

But there's no movement from inside and I can't hear anything. Well, that's not quite true. I hear *something*. It takes me a moment to place it, and I'm not even sure I've got it right. But it sounds wet, almost like someone smacking their lips. Only, that's not quite right.

Slurping?

I decide that's it. Maybe she's in there sucking spaghetti through her lips. It doesn't explain why the door's hanging open, though.

I step to the door and rap twice; it swings inward a bit as I do.

"Chera?" I call and curse my croaking voice. I clear my throat and call again.

No answer. The slurping sounds continue.

I step in, my heart hammering. What am I doing? This was a terrible idea. Unannounced, a secret admirer showing up with flowers on Valentine's, all because of a Facebook post.

I round into the living room and can see the kitchen beyond. The slurping is louder. I call her name again but am answered with only more slurping. I move closer to the kitchen.

That's when I see a foot—*her foot?*—on the floor. It slides out of sight a second later.

"Chera?" I ask, laying the flowers on a lampstand as I enter the kitchen.

Her face is gone, replaced by a wet and oozing crater. I try to scream but cannot. My lungs have seized and my throat is closed.

Over her corpse is the biggest Venus Flytrap I've ever seen, its barbed, toothy foliage dripping with gore as it consumes her. It has no eyes, yet still it stares at me.

Then I see the note, spattered with blood, lying on the floor. It reads: *Happy Valentine's Day, cunt. Here's a fucking plant.*

As the monstrous plant devours my secret crush, my lungs and throat loosen, and I am finally able to scream.

The Beekeeper by Alexander Shedd

It wasn't just the buzzing that drove her away, that infernal hum of a thousand apiformic drones which irritated her eardrums and scrambled her thoughts. It was the buzzing, and the fact that she suspected he never really listened to her anyway.

It had not been easy to date a sentient swarm of bees, but for two years she had made it work against all odds. Her friends told her he was no good, that he was bad news, that he was literal bees, but she never listened. She never thought he was capable of it. She thought he would die trying.

"I'm bumblebees, baby, I could never hurt you," he would coo in his sweet sussurant way. She believed him at the time, for far too long, but in the end she just had to accept that he was not bumbles at all but honeybees; he could lay on the sweet when he wanted, but when she really needed him, her friends were right. She would just get stung.

And now, alone on Valentine's Day, she sat in silence on the living room sofa, which was still covered in mesh, the way he liked it. Her wine was too dry and in her melancholy she thought of honey. She had not yet grown used to the new silence around the house. Despite herself, part of her longed to hear the overwhelming din of her boyfriend wandering through their home. She missed the flowers he would bring her, and the floral perfumes, though they often were mostly for him.

Suddenly, a knock at the door—no, not a knock, a thousand tiny knocks, the rising sound of infatuated insects throwing themselves at her door, politely, but determinedly.

"Honey," cried a thousand familiar little voices, "please open the door. I just want to talk."

Perhaps it was the hope that things could get better, that deep desire she had for him to be a better swarm to her and to himself, to really make this house their hive, but against her better judgment, she stood and walked to the door. Her hand hesitated on the knob.

"I don't know, Jason," she said. "How do I know you won't hurt me again?"

"It's Valentine's Day," he buzzed back. "Old Man Valentine was the patron saint of beekeepers…all I'm asking is you give me another chance, and be *my* keeper again."

She waited another moment. "I don't know," she said softly.

"I brought you flowers. Lavender and peonies, just how you like them," he continued. "Just dinner. That's all I'm asking. Then if you don't want to try again, I'll be out of your bonnet for good." She smiled a little, and opened the door.

Clean Up Crew by Eleanor Merry

"This bitch looks like shit," Miller comments, the disgust in his tone evident as they stand in the doorway of the worn-down motel room.

"Yeah, well what did you expect? A fucking playboy bunny?" Brad laughs, stepping into the room.

Jokes aside, the two men stand there for a moment and take in the carnage that is literally strewn across the room. This is their job, so you'd think they'd be used to this kind of thing, but today is taking the cake as far as what their normal 'clean-up' requires.

"Fuck," Brad finally says, rubbing his hand against the back of his neck in a nervous tic. "I can't even tell if she was hot before this."

Miller wrinkles his nose in disgust but dutifully steps in as well, grateful for the bags they'd put on their feet.

Miller and Brad had been a team for the past three years now, cleaning up after various organizations that required first-rate assistance. They were discreet, thorough and had zero moral compass, making them most of the city underworld's first choice for clean-up crews. They had seen some disturbing, fucked up stuff in their days, but this was right up there with the worst of them.

"What's that on the bedside table?" Brad asks. Miller walks up and takes a closer look, taking careful steps to avoid the worst of the gore.

"Umm, maybe a liver? I don't know. Some organ or another."

"Was this guy trying to re-create fucking Jack the Ripper or something?"

"Kinda looks like it."

"Fuck. Alright, grab the garbage bags, let's get fucking moving."

"Man, I hate Valentine's day," Miller grumbles as he begins to pick up pieces of flesh off the floor.

"Tell me about it, I still have to go for dinner with my wife after this shit. I didn't get her anything so I know she's just gonna bitch and whine the entire time."

Miller only chuckles as they hurry through the clean-up.

* * *

"Happy Valentine's Day, babe," Brad says as he kisses his wife's cheek, sliding a small box in front of her.

"Oh honey, you shouldn't have!" Shelly exclaims as she tears into the box, revealing the small pendant underneath. She looks down and it and frowns.

"Brad, what the hell is this?"

"What do you mean, baby?" Brad replies as he nods at the waiter in thanks for the drink just delivered in front of him. He needs it.

"Well, for one thing, it's still got blood on it."

Brad's eyes widen slightly. Oops.

"And for another, it says 'To Brenda, Love Phil'. Brad, did you get this from work?" Shelly scolds.

"Yes," Brad replies sheepishly. Shelly narrows her eyes at him before tossing the box down and walking out of the restaurant. Sighing, Brad takes a deep sip of his drink.

"Man, I fucking hate Valentine's Day."

I Need You To Need Me by Lance Dale

I've never been a big hit with the ladies. For most of my life, Valentine's Day has just served as a reminder of how lonely I am. It showed up every year just to kick me in the ribs. That's why I was so excited to find that pink envelope in my mailbox on February 13th. There was a note inside from a 'secret admirer' who wanted to meet out on the old trail at midnight. The admirer claimed they had been watching me around the apartment complex. *I have a secret admirer? Was it Cindy from across the hall? Oh god, I hope so!* I was so excited that it didn't even cross my mind that this could all be bullshit. Even knowing what I know now, I probably would've made the same decision. I was so desperate. I needed to feel needed, regardless of the outcome.

I sat and watched the clock all day. The seconds seemed to tick by like hours. I wished I had a fast forward button. I picked the letter back up again. It smelled like perfume. It was the opposite of loneliness. It made me feel whole. I looked back at the clock and it was approaching 10:00 p.m. It was time for me to get ready.

I had to put on my second nicest shirt. I had already spilled coffee on my nicest one. That wasn't going to stop me though. I also lost my car keys. It was so strange; I always put them on the hook by the door. I thought I must have had a mental-lapse from all the excitement and misplaced them. Thinking back on it now, there were probably some forces at work trying to warn me not to leave the house. Unluckily for me, there were plenty of taxi services who would drive me to my final destination.

It was finally time and my heart raced as the cab arrived at the start of the old trail. I got out and headed down. At first, I thought I had been duped and no one was there, but then I heard a voice call my name. It was Cindy from down the hall. I was right! I started walking towards her and that's when I realized she was not alone. There were a bunch of people in robes all around her. What the fuck did I just walk in to? Then one of the robed figures asked me if I was a virgin. I didn't even know what to say, but Cindy answered for me. "Oh yeah, he's a virgin." Then something came crashing down on my head and the lights all went out.

So here I am, tied to some weird ass table. The robed people are standing all around me and chanting nonsense words and Cindy has a knife. This may seem like the worst fucking luck ever, but on the bright side, someone finally needs me on Valentine's Day.

A Dozen Red Roses by P.J. Blakey-Novis

I've had twelve girlfriends over twelve years. They just never knew I existed until it was too late. I find myself awkward around women so I figured the relationship would last longer if we didn't have much contact. In fact, the only contact would be whatever glimpses I could catch through bedroom windows, any 'accidental' bumping into one another at the supermarket, and whatever they would post online for anyone to see. I never chose anyone who was in a relationship already—that would be wrong!

I kept myself to the shadows for months each year, learning what I could about my loves, preparing for that special day of the year—Saint Valentine's Day. On that day, after all my research and obsession, I would announce my love for them. Of course, I had to be careful not to be seen by anybody else in case of rejection, so I would make my grand gesture in the early hours of February 14th.

They would invariably be asleep as I forced the lock on their front doors and entered their bedrooms, each time the same. Gently, I'd shake them from their slumber, presenting the expensive bouquet of a dozen red roses. All I wanted was the gratitude, the appreciation, but it never came.

Not one of those twelve women even accepted the flowers, preferring to scream instead. The knife I carried for protection became the only way to stop the noise but how I hated to do it. I cried as I slit their throats, crimson spraying across the discarded roses, only adding to the deep red.

Twelve years and twelve victims, if you can call them that. But I'm confident that the next one will work out, and Valentine's Day is just around the corner.

Sweethearts by Angela Glover

Molly rushed home to get started on her valentines for school tomorrow, excited to hand out the zombie cards she picked out. After dinner, Molly and her mom prepared snack bags with candy to go with the cards. Her mom held up a small black box of conversation hearts and said,

"I found these fun zombie sweetheart candies at the store today for your cards."

"My friends will love them!" said Molly.

"Great job on your cards. Now let's go get ready for bed, please," said her mom. Molly ran upstairs to get ready for bed and she excitedly thought about tomorrow as she fell asleep.

"Good morning class and happy Valentine's Day! Are we ready to hand out our cards?" asked Mrs. Jones. The children eagerly stood up from their desks to exchange cards.

"Whoa! Cool! Thanks!" said Johnny.

"Cool, zombies!" said Amber.

Molly smiled and walked back to her desk. The morning recess bell rang, and the kids lined up at the door holding their snack bags. Molly landed on six in hopscotch, freezing when she heard screaming from inside. Beside her, Amber began to scream too. Molly looked over to see Amber's skin turn dark brown and rip open, covering her clothes in blood and rotten flesh. She turned and ran toward the school doors to get back inside. Mrs. Jones was screaming and pulling on the doors when Johnny jumped on her back, tearing her throat with his teeth. Molly hid by a garbage can near the doors as other kids jumped on Mrs. Jones.

She peeked at the playground and saw many of her classmates acting crazy. Mike had a large hole in his stomach and was pulling out his own intestines. Jessie gouged out her own eyes and was eating one of them. Luke's skin looked like it was melting, and he was chewing it.

Zombies, she thought.

Molly pulled out the little black box of sweethearts from her pocket and looked at the candy. *Rot. Brains. I Chews U. I Like Ur Guts. Nom Nom Nom.*

No way, she thought.

Principal Matthews came bursting through the doors in a panic but was immediately greeted by the kids devouring Mrs. Jones. Molly scrambled through the door before it shut and ran home.

Molly ran inside, slamming the front door and startling her mom.

"Molly! Why are you home?" Her mom asked with wide eyes, "Are you hurt?!"

"I'm okay. The kids are sick!"

Molly's mom called the school twice with no answer, so she called the police. As they waited for the officers, Molly pulled out the little box of sweethearts and dropped one in her hand, a mischievous grin on her face.

"Mom, want one?"

Her mom looked down at her hand and said, "Sure honey. Thanks."

Her mom tossed a sweetheart in her mouth with 'Dead' written on it and Molly's grin grew wider.

That's Amore by M Ennenbach

Dean Martin sang softly in the background, something something pizza pie.

I added in my own loud, harsh voice, "That's Amore!"

I rubbed my hands on the coarse towel hanging off of the oven door handle. They were sticky. It seemed everything in the room was sticky at the moment. Between the chocolate bubbling slowly in the pan and the glitter that had entrenched itself everywhere, the kitchen was a complete mess.

I just smiled and hummed along with Deano. Romance was in the air, a thick copper-scented emotion that made my heart swell. I half stepped, half danced across the tiled floor to grab the knife from the wooden blocks. It glinted merrily in the candlelight that filled the room. I shoved my hand into the open corpse on the kitchen table and wrestled out the still warm heart. After setting it on the chopping board, I began to cube it. The large muscle was difficult to cut, with its odd shape and slippery nature, but I am nothing if not persevering, and I managed the task. Then, I slid the quivering hunks onto the metal rods.

As I dipped them into the chocolate, I let out another rousing, "That's Amore!" and set them on the parchment paper to dry before packing them into the handmade heart that glinted with ribbon and glitter on the counter.

That's Amore, indeed.

Mummy's Broken Heart by Joel R. Hunt

Daddy broke Mummy's heart. I heard Mummy say so. It must really hurt when your heart breaks because Mummy kept crying. It was like she had a poorly tummy, except worse. She held Daddy's phone and screamed at him, asking who the women were that he had been talking to. Daddy said he didn't know any of them. That must be why Mummy was so mad at him. You aren't supposed to talk to strangers.

Daddy left and Mummy phoned Grandma. That was when she said about her broken heart. I don't think Mummy wanted me to hear, but I did. It made me very sad. I wanted to help her fix it, but I don't know how to fix a heart. Last year, Uncle Paul went to the hospital because his heart was hurting, and the doctors fixed it for him. Now he's all better.

I would like to be a doctor when I grow up.

Mummy was still crying when she put me to bed. I couldn't get to sleep because she forgot to read me a story, but I didn't tell her because then she would have felt worse.

It was dark when Daddy came back. He and Mummy started to argue about the strange women and about Mummy's broken heart. I didn't hear everything they said, but they used lots of bad words. I didn't like it at all.

Then Mummy screamed, and they both stopped shouting.

I don't like it when Mummy screams. It makes me scared. But I was glad that they weren't arguing anymore. I waited for them to come up to my room and tell me it was all better now, but they didn't. Everything downstairs was quiet.

I decided to go and see. I put on my bunny slippers which are my favourite

19

and I went down the stairs. The light was on in the kitchen. Daddy was sat against the wall holding a knife. He looked very scared, and he was looking at Mummy lying on the floor. She looked like Uncle Paul did when we visited him in the hospital before he got better. I think Daddy was trying to fix Mummy's broken heart like the doctors had done with Uncle Paul.

I asked Daddy if Mummy was okay. He jumped and threw his knife away. Then he took me out of the kitchen and back to my room. He told me Mummy was fine. She was just resting. Uncle Paul had to rest for a long time when his heart was fixed, so this made me happy because Mummy was getting better. When I was back in bed, Daddy went downstairs and made us both a drink.

It tastes funny, but he says I have to finish the whole cup. He says everything is going to be okay. He says me and him and Mummy will be together again soon.

I'm glad he was able to fix Mummy's broken heart.

I'm lucky to have such a clever Daddy.

The Last Love by Terry Miller

Roses wilt, wither, and fall from their places leaving behind nothing but their stems, wrought with thorns. How fitting that the aftermath of love's beauty be haunted by prickly reminders of the pain that it leaves behind! Cupid is a sick bastard with a demented sense of humor, his arrows dipped in deceptive poisons. Nothing could make Tiffany happier than to hold him down and pick off his cherub wings feather by feather while relishing in the screams of his anguish; such a perfect punishment for his cruel jokes on her ever-hurting heart.

He was surprisingly taller than Tiffany expected him to be but still quite short in comparison to herself. Cupid stood approximately three feet tall. Too bad his arrows could not free him from the chains. She examined their tips, the aroma stirring desires deep within her. Love and lust are said to be separated by a thin line but perhaps the secret ingredient to make one not the other lies in the fragrant coating of his arrows, whatever it may be.

Tiffany wondered if he had ever loved. Surely if he had, he would empathize and put down his evil bow once and for all. No, she's certain he simply took pleasure in the suffering of humankind. Perhaps that's the thing with God, gods, goddesses, angels, and the like; mere entertainment we are.

Cupid stared at her from his cell, his chains weighing heavy on his limbs. Tiffany opened the door, walked toward him, and drew a blade from her pocket. Its shiny tip traced his neck but he refused to flinch, either calling her bluff or immune to fear. She pressed the sharpened edge to his neck, then cut a gash inches across as his blood began to pour from the wound.

The basement filled with the aroma of the arrows' tips as he bled out.

21

Tiffany was struck with a dizzying intoxication, her nostrils taking in the scent that emanated from his emptying veins. She looked upon him with such adoration, tears welling up and falling from their ducts. She had never known such love in all her years, such beauty in one being. *What had she done?*

Cupids Bite by Trisha McKee

Shirley glanced over her shoulder and saw Frank staring.

Her heart flipped before she turned away, her mother's frenzied warnings reverberating in her head. Shirley understood the reserve needed when it came to matters of the heart.

She should have been braced against those butterflies in the stomach, those swooning sensations. She grew up in a world without dances, without romantic movies, without dinner dates. As a child, she had listened to her mother and aunts reminisce about being courted with flowers and poetry, indulging in all-night talks and kisses, sometimes slowly falling in love, sometimes tumbling quickly into passion.

And Shirley envied them those experiences. She resented the fact that they got to fall in love while she had to run the opposite way if a guy's gaze lingered. She wanted the flowers and fireworks, the first kiss and cuddles, even the awkwardness of getting to know one another.

"Shirley?"

She jumped. "Frank! Hi." The surprise lifted her voice to an unnaturally high pitch. "What's up?"

"I…I wondered if we could go over the notes for Art History."

"I'm not sure that's a good idea." In high school, the teachers had worked to keep girls and boys separated. But in college, it was assumed everyone would make the right decisions.

Frank nodded, his eyes on her lips as he licked his own. "Sure, but…just to go over notes."

She finally agreed, following him to an empty room, not protesting when he scooted his chair closer to her.

"You're so beautiful," he whispered, his fingers trembling as they danced up her arm. "We're safe in here. Hidden."

His words were cut off abruptly by a pounding on the wall, a pounding so intense the room shook. The air thickened, the butterflies in Shirley's stomach turned to lead, and the couple jumped apart with startled yelps.

As the lights flickered, Shirley stood. "He's here. Dammit."

"Be quiet! Maybe—"

But the door flew open, and in flew Cupid, his teeth bared, a deep growl warning the couple of his intentions. His eyes flashed red, and he drew his arm back, an arrow with blood dripping from its tip clenched in his fat fist.

Shirley backed up until she was against the wall, not believing the sight in front of her. She had grown up knowing that Cupid had contracted some severe strain of rabies, but she had not realized how quickly he could find and destroy. She thought it was simply a scare tactic adults used to scare the younger ones and keep them from testing the legend.

But as Cupid circled them before finally closing in on her, she realized it was all very true. He was still alerted to potential love, but instead of arriving to help it along, he showed up to attack. And as he sunk his fangs into her neck, Frank's screams echoing in her dimming mind, she wished she had at least gotten a first kiss out of the whole experience.

Tunnel O' Love by P.J. Blakey-Novis

It was supposed to be romantic; a trip to the fairground on Saint Valentine's Day. The kids were with their grandparents so that Maria and I could have some quality time. I should have thought it through.

I don't like heights, or rides at all, really, but I tried to make the effort. Maria dragged me onto the Ferris wheel, and I was petrified.

She laughed at me.

I spent a small fortune trying to win a stuffed toy for Maria, but everyone knows those games are rigged.

She laughed at me again.

I tried not to let it bother me, but the guy next to me managed to hit all the coconuts, his girlfriend squealing with pride as he handed her a cuddly elephant. Maria muttered something about being "a real man." She spotted the Tunnel O' Love, a short trip through a tunnel on a rowboat which would afford us a few moments to make out like teenagers.

We took our seats and Maria asked if I was going to get seasick. She'd gone beyond innocent mockery to full-on bitch and I'd had enough. We floated through the tunnel for less than five minutes, but it was long enough for me to squeeze the life out of her and dump her in the shallow water.

Secret Romance by Galina Trefil

Kate had never enjoyed the company of men much—not the living ones anyway. But, unlike the majority of the female population, she had never been so close-minded as to consider living a requirement for romance.

It was a difficult truth to bear alone. She wanted to discuss her proclivities as freely as anyone else, but she knew that if she said a word her friends would stop speaking to her, and her family, well, geez, they might even try to get her committed. Just the word "necrophile…" it had such terribly unfair connotations. The sound of it made her skin crawl and her guts wobble with confused humiliation. She understood easily enough why the world condemned people like her as perverts, even if she didn't agree.

Why did she love death? She didn't know. It was just the way that she had always been. She wasn't proud of it and it certainly hadn't made her life easier. She'd tried dealing with the other kind of men, the ones that were room temperature, and, nope, she just couldn't force her body to have that spark, that same intense physical reaction that ran through her when she placed her palms against peaceful, passive, cool remains. The submissive remains which would never stand her up, never yell at her or cheat on her, never make a mess of her apartment, never snore immediately after sex, never forget to lower the toilet seat.

"You need to get out more," one of her colleagues at the forensic lab urged her. "Come on. Valentine's Day is coming up. You can't be alone for that."

"I won't be," she replied, smoothing clay across the handsome skull of a John Doe that some hikers had found up in the mountains the week before. "I've got my work."

"Work won't get you orgasms, girl."

Oh, yes it will, Kate thought to herself. Truly, it was far from an accident that she'd gotten into the business of facial reconstruction. She was good at her job too. The finished face that she molded onto the head led to its identification and motive for murder a week after it was shown on the news.

Kate clipped a photo of the deceased young mortician for her album at home. God, he'd been gorgeous before he'd been killed. But more gorgeous afterwards.

"Tell me your story," she murmured to the photo. "It's okay to talk to me. Believe me, I understand."

"They caught me," the mortician's image whispered to her. "The mortuary put video cameras up and didn't tell me about it. On the slab, that lady was just so pretty...I couldn't resist.... After I got caught, the mortuary fired me and told her family. The husband refused to let bygones be bygones...so I wound up in the mountains."

"At least it brought us together," Kate sighed.

"Don't ever let them catch you too."

"Don't worry," she promised, kissing the picture of the skull. "I can keep a secret."

Cassandra by Chris Bannor

She dreamed of the end of days the way some men dreamed of women. Longing filled her blood and devotion made her scream out the death of thousands. No one believed her, the sobbing woman who begged on street corners and told them to repent. The end of days would come, and the darkness would rise from the depths.

When His call came, those who heard it would be no more likely to survive His arrival than any other. It was sweet to her though, and death at His hands was the caress of a lover's kiss to her soul.

When The Night Has Come by Tina Merry

Why am I waiting? It's time.

Yesterday I thought I knew everything. Now, my thoughts are in a shadow again. A wisp of steam. A murmur barely heard. The light goes on, then off.

It starts with silly mind games, playing out in my head. Something said, something implied; a whisper of a thought, or at least a thought which is to be implied. Is there a difference, in the end? Whether we imply, or infer, or expose the truth in all it's ugly baldness, does it change the result?

He promised we'd be together forever. He lied, she lied, and the worst sin of all was I lied to myself.

I walked out the backdoor of our remote farmhouse in the early dusk, reflecting on the irony of my husband's decision that we obtain a few pigs. A pig for the pigs? Perhaps.

Chuckling, I sauntered over to barn from which loud rock music was blaring out. As I reached the door, it stopped. I paused in shock, wondering why. The old boom box was plugged in, and the light above the barn door was on, indicating power, so there was no obvious reason for the sudden silence which seemed to descend in the yard.

Goosebumps crawled up the back of my neck and my hand shook as I reached hesitantly for the doorknob, willing myself to be able to see through the solid door.

At that moment, I heard a sharp crash, plus other strange grunting sounds

29

which didn't make sense. I pulled my hand back sharply and turned to pick up the hand axe beside the door.

The music began again, this time no longer loud rock. Instead, I hear **Imagine**. John Lennon, our wedding song. I tried to shake the fog from my brain, seeking to make sense of everything happening. I stood there what felt an eternity but was probably only a few minutes. Finally, I swung open the door, with the axe raised above my head, and stood in shock, staring at the macabre scene before me.

"Hi baby, I missed you", my husband said as he reached out for my hand. "May I have this dance?"

Numb fingers dropped the axe in my raised hand, as I sunk to my knees in horror.

He'd obviously had lots of time to prepare. The slut had been dismembered, her body parts gathered into a wheelbarrow, and the air was thick with the smell of blood. He'd cleaned himself up of most of the blood, but I could see the saw he'd used, and a large pile of bloody rags.

As my husband stepped forward to help me stand up, my head began to clear again. Yes, this was all good. Everything would be alright again. The first few notes of Imagine began once more as he pulled me into his arms for our dance.

All is forgiven, and our night has come.

The Mate Of Her Desires by DJ Elton

"Only four drops twice a day," Marel had said. "Any more than that won't work. Or you'll feel sick."

Carrie was intrigued. As much as she loathed taking traditional medicine, this method seemed pretty harmless, no side effects. Besides, Marel seemed to know all about herbs, lotions and potions, witch that she was.

She felt excited, if not a little embarrassed, and decided to put the potion into action. After all, it had been an entire week now. The blend should be working. Carrie had been in bed with the flu the past couple of days, but had been diligently taking the drops as part of her healing regimen.

"I want to attract the mate of my desires," she had told Marel. This in itself had been a bold confession. She was not able to be more specific in her request than that. Marel had concocted the brew, assuring Carrie she would get all she wished for.

Carrie drove to a local café and sat on a high stool, ordering a cappuccino. A pimply young man with a guitar over one shoulder sat down on a nearby chair.

"It's me, Carrie. I've come to massage your shoulders, then play you a song." He proceeded to do just that. Next, a middle-aged woman sat down on the opposite chair, facing Carrie.

"Hi, darling. I've come to hand feed you your favorite chocolate mud cake." She started to spoon the cake next to Carrie's coffee into her mouth. "Eat it, sweetheart," she winked.

Suddenly there were not two, but six people surrounding Carrie in the café. One man was playing with her hair, taking it out of its clip and sifting his hands through her long brown mane. Another was kneeling beside her stroking her legs with a touch as light as a feather. Another was caressing her arms. Another was whispering sweet talk in her ear and attempting to kiss her on the lips.

"Too much!" she screamed. "Please go away." But they were all oblivious to each other and the sounds of protest Carrie was making. She eventually stopping crying out when they carried her into the nearby woods, where it was quieter and much more spacious.

Only then did Carrie realize all that she had wished for was literally happening. All at once. Marel's magic drops were doing their work.

A Final Valentine by Andrea Allison

She sat by his hospital bed for two days, her hand in his. He grew colder as each hour passed. His breath came in dribs and drabs. His weary eyes looked into hers. His voice only a whisper.

"I…got you a Valentine's gift, my dear. The last…one it seems. On my workbench in the gara…. It's what you deserve." He closed his eyes and drifted off, allowing death to embrace him.

She felt numb wandering home after losing this man she loved so suddenly. The last piece of his love sat waiting for her. A brown box sitting among scattered tools. She stared at it for a moment before lifting the cardboard flaps. Only a jar nestled inside. Bewildered, she lifted it high up by the lid, examining it in the light. Her heart stopped, seeing another floating in clear liquid.

A piece of paper fell to the bench as the jar slipped from her fingers, landing on a hammer. Trembling, she reached for the note, unfolding it.

Since you had an overwhelming desire to stop my heart, I decided to cut your beloved sister's out as fair trade. Or should I say, my wife. Yeah, I knew. It was fun while it lasted. The damage of your poison did its job but at least I got a parting gift, murdering little twins won't be playing their reindeer games on anymore unsuspecting future suitors. You walk this planet alone now. Cuddle with your jar.

Happy Valentine's Day!

P.S. I left everything to my crazy aunt who eats hair. Ha Ha.

Bite Me By Kevin J. Kennedy

Three months we were dating, and we still hadn't slept together.

"I'm not like other girls," she would always say.

Valentine's Day was the big day, or night anyway.

After dinner we went back to her place. As she undressed, I could see she had made the effort. Matching red bra and panties. She had even worn red stockings with bows.

I dove on her, kissed her all over and then ripped her panties off.

I almost fell off the bed when I saw her pussy had teeth.

"I won't bite you, I promise."

"I like being bitten," I responded.

Blood Wine by Sea Caummisar

Jarod was sweet enough to hold the door open as Sandra entered the restaurant. This was his first date since his girlfriend moved out six months ago and he wanted to be sure to do everything perfectly. It wasn't every day that he met a woman on the internet that interested him. Especially with Valentine's Day being their first date, he knew there was pressure to be a perfect gentleman.

As she walked in, Sandra wrinkled her nose. "What is this place again? What am I smelling?"

The hostess interrupted Sandra as she took their reservation and led them to a table. In Sandra's eyes the place was too dark and unsettling.

As he sat down, Jarod began explaining himself. "A friend told me about this place. It's only open two nights a year: Valentine's Day and Halloween. I saw on your dating profile that you also love old vampire movies. My friend told me about this place and said it's the best."

Sandra fought the urge and repressed her feelings of wanting to run out of the place. Of course she had to pick a blind date with a guy that only noticed her interest in vampires on her profile. She knew it was risky using a horror dating website, but she also liked the thrill of it.

The already dimmed lights got darker. Nearly naked women covered in red body paint took to the stage. Once again, Sandra caught a whiff of a familiar aroma. The women on stage started wiggling their bodies. They reached in between their legs and scooped out menstrual blood from their vaginas and rubbed it on each other.

A worker approached their table and set down two wine glasses. "As you can see, I brought two clean needles, unopened. I am licenced to take blood. So, will you be drinking your own or each other's?"

Nothing was making sense to Sandra.

"Our own. First date." Jarod nodded.

Still confused, Sandra watched as the worker plunged the needle in her date's arm and let his red fluid drain into his own wine glass. She had to fight the urge to flee, because she was feeling her eye teeth start to grow, something she refused to show in public.

Jarod was smiling, but his eyes weren't glowing like his date's red eyes.

He saw his date wasn't smiling. "Too much for you? Is it too over the top? I thought this would impress you."

In the darkness of the room, Sandra allowed her teeth to grow longer. Sandra bit into her wrist and let her own blood flow into her own wine glass. Sandra gave her offering to Jarod.

Jarod had actually impressed her. This was a mortal she wouldn't mind sharing her immortality with.

He almost wet his pants as he realized his date was an actual vampire.

All Dolled Up by Trish McKee

Penny set the plate down, sighing as she made her way around the table to her chair. "Not sure why Valentine's Day is in such a dreary, cold month. Nothing romantic about February, but I guess at our age romance isn't as important, right, Russ?"

She scooted her chair in and then glanced across the table. He merely stared down at his plate. "Now, come on. I didn't put anything fancy in it. Just sauce and pasta, not a lot of spices. Just as you like it." She reached for the bread basket. "Here, have a roll. I'll butter it for you. But anyways, Shandra is having her Valentine's party. Well, you know that. We're not invited. It's amazing how selfish your children can be when you're not in a position to give them anything. Right?"

There was a long pause, and she glanced up, her shoulders sinking. "Don't say it. I know. I'm being too hard on her. But to tell us we're not wanted…unless certain conditions. That's just shameful! It's not right, Russ, and I'm—I'm upset." She stopped, turning her head as tears fell, her fist pressed to her mouth. She shook her head to stop him from saying anything.

"Mom?" Shandra's voice rang out from the front entryway.

Penny widened her eyes and wagged a finger. "Russ, not a word. Okay? Let me handle this." She tilted her head back. "We're in the kitchen, Shandra."

Shandra strode into the room, her gaze skimming across the table before she shook her head and faced her mother. "Mom, c'mon. Come have dinner with us. Please. The kids miss you."

"Shandra! Enough! Do not treat your father like this! I won't tolerate it. I will not stand for you not speaking directly to him, and I sure as hell won't go to dinner without him."

Shandra dropped her head and pinched the bridge of her nose. "Mom. You cannot bring him. We've been through this. Please—"

"No! He has been nothing but the best father to you ungrateful kids—"

"Was! Mother, he was! He's been dead for six months. This—this has to stop." She made her way around the table and grabbed the mannequin. "You have to stop this or we'll have to get you some help."

Penny dove toward them, her scream echoing. "Don't hurt him! Don't hurt your father!"

She grabbed the mannequin from her daughter, sobbing as she held him close. "Russ, are you okay? I'm sorry. I'm so sorry. I never knew she would attack you!"

"Mom—"

"Get out!" She fixed the mannequin back into the chair, tucking the napkin into his shirt. Glancing over her shoulder, Penny yelled, "I said get out!" As her daughter made her way out of the house, Penny whispered, "I'm sorry, my love. It's terrible, how they treat us. Just awful. But we have each other. Happy Valentine's, husband."

Teddy by Archit Joshi

You're used to this, he told himself. *You've been lonely all your life.*

But this was different. It was the "season of love" as they call it, and he had no one. He writhed in an armchair. At the other end of the room, she sat in her rocking chair, shooting him with wordless disapproval.

"What, you don't like her?" He pointed a blameful finger towards her unmoving body. "It's getting harder and harder to please you."

She didn't respond. His fingers dug into the faux leather of his armchair. She meant well. Couldn't bear to see him without someone to love, especially when the magical 14th was just around the corner. Calming down, he tenderly walked over to her and knelt down. He took her hand in his. The flesh had decayed away by now, and her brittle bones felt rough against his palm. Soon, he would have to remove the bandages. Opt for something more complex…perhaps embalming.

He stayed there until his frustration dissipated and then made for the stranger on his bed. She'd bled all over his bed sheets, the bitch. Leaning over her, Ted could see why his girlfriend didn't approve of this one. Her hair was just right: long, brunette, with a perfect part in the middle. Both their heights matched too. But this one was chubby, and death wasn't a good look on her. She wouldn't fit easily into her trunk. His hacksaw would be put to good use later. But before that, he had work to do.

He angled the dead bimbo's body so its head faced towards his sweet girlfriend.

You rejected this one, just like your Papa rejected me. Now you get to watch.

He unbuckled his pants.

* * *

"Fuck!" Lynda kicked her car. Sunlight was retreating from the long winding roads and there were rumors of wild coyotes in the surrounding woods. No cell service. David was waiting at home, probably ready with exquisite surprises for their first Valentine's.

Sudden headlights blinded her. Shielding her eyes, she saw a Volkswagen Beetle approaching. It stopped a few feet away, and a man got out. He was tall and handsome, with defiantly wavy hair. Strangely enough Lynda felt a sense of comfort by his mere presence.

"Car trouble?"

"Yeah. Bummer. Say, could you give me a lift into the city?"

He seemed harmless enough.

The man hesitated. "I'm actually going the other way…."

"Please? I have someone waiting for me at home."

His face eventually lit up with a charming smile.

"Fine, I'll give you a lift."

* * *

He started with her purpling lips, seductively moving downwards. After death, and before *rigor mortis*. Perfect sweet spot. Halfway through, he glanced at his girlfriend in her rocking chair, searching her eyes for a hint of approval. There was only reproach. Seeing this, he went soft.

"Now *she's* not good enough for you?!" Fuming, he abandoned the naked corpse. Putting on his shirt, he reached again for his hacksaw.

Valentine's for Gods and Monsters by Joshua E. Borgmann

"Doesn't sitting here among all these lovers make you regret what you gave up?" Circe asked as she took a drink of her wine.

Eros smiled. "I may not go around spreading love anymore, but I love the two of you dearly." He sipped his vodka and placed a hand on each woman's leg.

"What about Lily?" the mousy woman in dark glasses and a baseball cap asked.

Eros sipped his drink again and said, "In a certain way, but she's your girlfriend, M."

Circe giggled, "The two of you have gotten pretty intimate in bed, my love."

"What do you expect when four people share a bed? It doesn't change the fact that she's a bit too immaterial for me."

"Different partners for different reasons," M said, nonchalantly shoving an oddly twisting braid back under her cap.

Staring out across the bar, Circe took in the large Valentine's Day crowd. She noticed Lily with her blood-red hair talking to a man in a cheap black suit. She smiled and said, "She's made contact."

"Are you ready?" Eros asked.

As if on cue, the three of them watched as 'cheap black suit' walked off to the bathroom.

Circe got up and pulled a vial from her purse as she walked toward Lily. Aside from the four of them, no one noticed her depositing the contents of the vial in 'cheap suit's' drink.

Thirty minutes later, 'cheap suit' was escorting Lily out the door. Eros, Circe, and M followed at a discrete distance. It was best to let the prey think he was still the hunter. A few yards down the street, he pushed Lily into an alley. By the time, the three lovers caught up, he was already slitting her throat.

For a few seconds, he looked happy, but then Lily evaporated.

"Not what you were expecting," Eros growled, and the Valentine's Day Slasher turned to face a man in a long leather trench coat, a beautiful woman in a red dress, and a nerdy girl in a unicorn shirt.

"What…" Before he could finish, the girl in the unicorn shirt took off her glasses to reveal the most stunningly beautiful silver eyes. He was lost in them and became like a statue of himself.

Eros approached the killer and pulled the man's face toward his. Still frozen from Medusa's brief gaze, he couldn't look away as Eros fed him back all the pain that he had caused each of his seventeen victims. He felt the terror of his every knife slash and was left weeping on the ground.

"Your turn," Eros said, and Circe whispered, "Wallow."

Where the weeping killer had been now was a hog.

Lilith rematerialized behind the pig and slit his throat with his own knife. As the dying animal squealed, she whispered, "Serves you right, you swine."

Then, drenched in blood, she turned to her lovers and said, "Now, can we have a well-deserved Valentine's Day celebration?"

The four hunters walked off into the night.

Lonely Hearts Dance by N.M. Brown

No one's exactly sure when the meetings began,
   We just knew we were grateful and all formed a plan.
   A group for survivors and current victims of stalking,
   We longed for safety at home, at work, while out walking.
   We would convene, share horrors and vent,
   Well assured they would come, in their minds we paid rent.
   It was my idea to use the barn for Valentine's Day,
   We would reach out to them and then lure them away.
   The Lonely Hearts Dance, the name that we give it,
   To be a beautiful, decorated proverbial snake pit.
   Our obsessors were contacted (the ones not convicted),
   We told them our hearts were no longer conflicted.
   We told them to meet us for a Valentine's date,
   Offering ourselves, for a purpose, as bait.
   We all have various methods, luring tales and lies,
   I insist I drive him in my car, telling him there's a surprise.
   His eyes twinkled with joy, hands restless and fumbling,
   Surprised to finally have me, his words he was mumbling.
   I leaned in, listened and laughed when he spoke,
   His breath on my face, my disgust made me choke.
   We arrived at the barn, not the first ones there,
   I enticed him inside, right into my snare.
   My arm in his arm, I distracted him with punch,
   He blissfully drank it, not so much as a hunch.

Their vile hands yearning, affections toxic like sewers,

After the first dance we broke away from our pursuers.

The door was locked up, trapping them all inside,

Panic we heard, no shadows for them left to hide.

I threw the first match, Collin Rhett threw the next,

The flames spread fast, their screaming voices perplexed.

I stood close by, nearly seared from fire's breath,

The noise faded inside as each one met their death.

Reclaiming our lives in a victorious raze,

A life of being hunted had reached the end of its days.

The group breathed easy, all with burned valentines,

But there was one lone survivor…one stalker…. It's mine.

She's Trouble by Kevin J. Kennedy

I always had a thing for panties. I'd rather have sex with a girl who kept hers on than one who was totally naked.

I had gone out to a club on Valentine's Day as I was single and feeling a bit low. I reasoned pulling a random and sleeping with them was better than being alone.

It hadn't taken long to pull, then we were in a taxi back to her place.

She was everything I wanted. She had kept her panties on but got another pair from the drawer and given me a hand job with them. I've only ever read about panty jobs, but it was amazing. While the pair she wore were red lace and mainly see through, she used a white silk pair to rub up and down my member.

I laidback with my hands behind my head and watched her work. She smiled up at me.

She stood up on the bed and slipped the panties down her legs. I was a little disappointed to be honest, but when she knelt back down over my chest and began to slip them into my mouth, I got all the harder. I was in heaven. She moved back down my body and I began to feel woozy. At first, I thought it was the alcohol, and then the room started to spin and sway way worse than I had ever experienced. I knew I hadn't drunk that much. I hadn't been out that long.

"It's okay baby, go to sleep."

It was hours later when I awoke tied to the bed.

"What the fuck?" I called out.

"Shhh!" I heard come from my side. I spun my head round to see the girl from the night before sitting in the chair. She looked even hotter than I remembered her, which was the reverse of what usually happened when the beer goggles wore off.

"What did you do to me? Why am I tied to the bed?"

"Well, you are tied to the bed because I need to keep you here until I drain all of your life force. I didn't do much to you but when I slipped my panties into your mouth, the scent knocked you unconscious. I have what some may describe as a poison pussy. Like all predators, it's my weapon. I suppose most women could say that, but in my case, it's a little more accurate."

"What the fuck are you talking about, you psycho!?"

"Shhhh, darling. Go back to sleep."

And with that she stood and pulled a pair of her panties over my head. The room began to spin again. As I was passing out, I heard her say, "Pussy always gets men into trouble, baby."

Muse by Andra Gill

Satine squeezed the ventricle. Blood seeped between her fingers, pattering down onto the canvas like raindrops. It had surprised her that his heart was no larger than his fist, its weight less than a bag of his favorite French roast coffee.

"Heartbreak is an artist's great muse, right?" He'd thrown his arms wide as he yelled. His lips that had once roused her to passionate heights now curled into a sneer. "Well, you've broken my heart. Use that as your masterpiece."

Satine had taken him at his word.

A pulpy crimson clot oozed out and landed with a wet splash.

Graveyard Lover by Ximena Escobar

She walked among the gravestones, seeking the chill that usually preceded the fog. As branches swayed in the dirty white sky, her back bristled cold. Then came the high-pitched ringing in her ear, and the force that squeezed the ache between her legs. Her arms were pulled up by an invisible strength, bracelets of redness circling her wrists.

Her toes took off from the cool moist ground; like Ophelia in a stream of air, she drifted over the graveyard. There it emerged, hovering over her forehead. Opening her mouth, she let the grey wind gag her. Rising, she climaxed....

Until next time.

A Good Pounding by Scott Deegan

She knelt next to the dumpster behind the bar on 5th street. Brock stood in front of her, his pants halfway down his thighs. This is how he got off these days. The case was too high profile for any decent girl to want to date him.

He'd lost his place on the swim team as well, despite his father's best efforts. At least he didn't have to register as a sex offender. Had the case actually made it to trial he may have had to wear that moniker for the rest of his life. He could never let anyone who knew him see him getting sex from a meth head.

Today was Valentine's Day, and he wasn't going to let the anniversary of the day that little tramp had played him, and then passed out before following through, go by without some kind of celebration. When the woman on her knees finished servicing him, he pulled up his jeans and tucked himself in. She had just started to get up when he struck her head with the bottle he'd taken from the trash. She fell back against the brick wall using her hands to keep from totally collapsing in the alleyway. She would have made it too, had he not pistoned his knee into her face. Her nose exploded in a spray of blood and her teeth, already rotting from the drugs, broke and scattered across the macadam. He knelt beside her, caressing her broken face as he repeatedly thrust the jagged end of the bottle between her legs and into her sex.

"Call me a rapist you little bitch, will you? You know you like it. You wanted it, didn't you?" he asked as her body finally gave up resisting and she accepted her fate.

Emily had found Brock by accident when he passed her New Year's Eve, leaving a bar about three blocks from the one he stood behind tonight. After what he did to her and the trial, she realized just how little thought he gave to the girls he violated. He had actually run into her, even had the audacity to ask her out. Not once did he show any signs of knowing who she was. She knew him. She would never forget waking up to see his face contorted in a mixture of hate and lust as he used her unconscious body for his sexual gratification.

Her father worked in road construction, so when she found the tool in the back of his truck she practiced with it. Acclimated herself to the weight and operation of it. He hadn't heard her approach, he was so engrossed in the scene before him. The baseball bat laid him out cold.

He awoke to find her standing over him in a place he didn't know. His legs were spread and tied to wooden rafters but his back was on the floor. He was naked from the waist down, or up, as the case may be.

Emily stepped between his upstretched legs and hefted the tool. She placed the tip on his anus and he felt it start to sink in from the sheer weight of it. His eyes widened in terror as Emily gently squeezed the trigger of the jackhammer.

The Date by Aindrila Roy

There's this guy I met at work that set my heart beating. There was something about him that pulled me to him. An inexplicable attraction. I often wondered what it was about him. Was it the broad shoulders? Or maybe the long, artistic fingers were the reason. Perhaps it was the sharp nose. His angular jaws could be the culprit too. I never could figure it out. What I did know was that I wanted him.

He was unlike any of my previous dates; each was a saga of failed expectations. Honestly, I had begun to wonder if it was me. One or two still made sense, but seven? The fault had to be with me, right? But then he came, and I knew. I knew fault lay with them, not me. They were not *him.*

It had not been easy. He did play hard to get, but I was unrelenting. He was all I ever wanted. After a long, and frankly a tiresome pursuit, he was finally here. As my date. On Valentine's Day, no less. On the day of love, I would be having a little celebration of my own.

I straightened my dress a little nervously. Swallowing my nervousness, I opened the door, shivering a little at the cold air that hit me. Stepping into the room, my eyes were drawn to where he sat. I gave a small smile and walked over. I had planned an elaborate date, mainly because he was not much of a planner. I, on the other hand, am an obsessive planner. Even the slightest misstep can drive me into a maddening frenzy. The fevered rage that haunted me while I was pursuing my current date is the latest example, but…I digress.

I smoothed a crease on my dress and walked over to where he sat, waiting.

"Hi darling," I said and bent down to kiss his cold lips.

It was perfect. He was perfect. Tonight would be perfect. Tonight, I would *finally* get my dreams. Our mating would be like I always imagined. He was exactly how I liked my men – Cold. Unmoving. Dead.

New Heart by James Pyles

Helena was determined to rebuild her love, even if it killed him.

She once wanted to be a doctor, but her Mom told her she should be a nurse. Her Dad said she should go to a trade school, someplace to meet a guy, settle down and get married.

The white wedding dress she dreamed of when she was nine eventually frayed, became soiled, and then was soaked in blood.

"Don't worry, Jeremy." The smile on her pale face was more of a grimace, and dark, curly hair, moist with sweat, fell into her eyes as she bent over him. "I'll make it right, don't worry." Her brown eyes filled with tears, but only for a moment. "You said you loved me. You told me you gave me your heart. Now you really will."

Scalpel and rib spreader in her hands, she continued to work. Fluid and flesh smeared all over her latex-covered hands as she deftly maneuvered needle and suture. "Two years of medical school before I washed out didn't go to waste, Jeremy," she muttered to her cold paramour. "Clerval may have been a quack who got thrown out of his teaching position, but he was also a damned genius." She went over the crude stitches in the organ which she'd managed to get beating, tightening up the leaks. "Before he committed suicide, thanks to my seducing him, he showed me his notebook. A year later, I met you."

Helena watched a vein throb in his throat and felt his skin start to warm. "I never thought I'd get to use the journal I'd taken from his corpse, but then you came along. You said you loved me and that you'd never leave me." She bit her lip enough to make it bleed, a drop trailing down her chin until it fell onto his still unmoving lips. "You lied!"

Raging, she wanted to hit him in the face with her fist, but his chest was still open, and anyway, that wasn't the plan.

"Funny how karma works. Car accident on a Friday night, and I'm the lousy coroner this weekend. I'll switch you for another cadaver. No one will know you were ever missing…or dead.

When she was done, his chest bore stitches like a football, but his skin was pink, and his lungs were filling with air.

"You're alive again, Jeremy, and this time you'll really never leave me. I've given you a new heart, and it, and everything else you have, belongs to me."

Quetzalcoatl's Valentine by Joshua E. Borgmann

What could be more romantic than a Valentine's Day cruise? I'd thought that when Dylan booked this trip, and as we sat down to a Valentine's Day lunch in the Windjammer Cafe, I was giddy with excitement for the rest of the day.

Yesterday, we'd had a wonderful day of excursions. We'd toured a tequila factory and drank many samples, and we'd taken a Jeep to see the Mayan pyramids. We'd gotten our drink and our culture on, and today was supposed to be all about romance. We'd have a quite lunch, spend some time at the pool, go to the couples' spa, have a nice dinner, and finish with dancing before retiring to our cabin for some private fun.

It was a dream that wasn't meant to be.

I was picking at a piece of salmon as Dylan finished off his second pork chop when I noticed a lot of people staring out the windows and pointing. The views were always great, so I expected it was maybe a school of dolphins. I wish it had been dolphins. Instead, I looked up to see a giant *thing* squirming in the sky about half a mile away. It looked like some kind of metallic snake with scales that gleamed in the sunlight. The scales looked like feathers. Yes, a great feathered serpent, I thought.

"Looks like that god they told us about, Questlove or Questcoyote," Dylan mumbled. "It must be some special attraction."

I tried to believe that was all it was. "It's not Questlove, silly. Quetzal-something…"

"Quetzalcoatl," I heard several people say. And I knew that was it.

Suddenly, twin beams of fire shot from the creature's mouth and engulfed both sides of the ship.

"What the hell?" Dylan said, finally pushing away his lunch.

"It's burning the lifeboats!" someone screamed.

People started for the exits, but there were too many of us. Where could we go anyway? We were all trapped on this ship at the thing's mercy. Could a thing like that have mercy? Certainly not, I thought, knowing that we were doomed. I wished that we'd stayed home and went to the Cheesecake Factory, but I feared I'd never eat cheesecake again.

I stared up at the thing as it suddenly dived straight toward us. I screamed as the glass shattered and ducked to the side. Dylan stood frozen until the creature's feathers ripped into him, turning him into a shower of gore. Then I was wearing my Valentine's Day date. Blood and bits of flesh dripped down my shirt, and something heavy landed in my hands. My screams turned to whimpers as I saw half of Dylan's heart caught between my fingers. I knew this ghoulish memento was to be my final valentine.

The floor beneath me was gone, and death was a gift I eagerly accepted as I fell into the twisted remains of our doomed ship, still clutching my beloved's dead heart.

Thirteen More by Chris Bannor

Theirs was a love that was never meant to be, not in the way of Hollywood stories and romance novels. There would never be an audience that would cheer them on, never a reader who would cry tears of joy at their longing gazes and lingering touches.

Their love was death.

As he watched the knife slide home, he smiled viciously at his lover. Multiple knife wounds bleed at their feet and the girl sobbed into her cloth gag.

There was only time for a quick kiss as he slipped his knife into their sacrifice one final time.

"Happy Valentine's."

Heart-Shaped Box by Alanna Robertson-Webb

Yesterday was Valentine's Day, and I woke up to find a worn, heart-shaped box on the pillow next to me.

This would be sweet if anyone else had been in my house, but I live alone in the middle of the woods.

My door and windows were still locked, and the only thing out of place was a set of large claw marks near the door handle.

I finally opened the box, and immediately had to vomit.

Inside were the ragged, bloody skins of several forest animals. They had unusual bite marks in them, and I'm terrified to step outside.

The Gift of a Heart by Aaron Channel

Serena awoke abruptly, her heart beating fast and hard, distributing a sudden burst of adrenaline throughout her body…. Her heart. She took a breath and revelled in the organ's strength. The rhythm of it, that brand new, perfect, healthy heart.

No more hospital rooms. No more doctors telling her to just hold on. No more dilated cardiomyopathy—the two words which had ruled her life until three short weeks ago.

Selena's musings were cut short as a thought worked its way up from her subconscious. She had been asleep, had woken up….

Danger!

Her brain barely connected the word with the half-remembered sound of her bedroom door opening before she was leaping from her bed, just one second too late. The sickly-sweet smell of the rag and the sound of a strange woman muttering to herself were the last things that Serena experienced.

Lillian talked to her late husband as she went about her important work.

"Don't worry, honey. We'll get you another chance. I promise." With great deliberation she placed the knife against Serena's temple and brought down her mallet with a horrible crunching sound.

"I know, love. It's risky, but don't worry. The damage to her frontal lobe will leave her a vegetable, but she can live for days like this, maybe even weeks. I didn't hurt any of the parts of her brain that deal with autonomic responses. I studied this very carefully." Now rifling through Serena's purse, Lillian carelessly discarded makeup and prescription bottles in her haste to get to Serena's wallet.

"Ha! See! I told you it would work. See the red dot on her ID? I knew she'd be an organ donor. Perfect."

Lillian had one final chore before she could leave. She picked up Selena's phone and carefully dialed 9-1-1.

"Hello? Operator? There is a woman here. I think she's dying. You'd better hurry." Three quick steps and she was to the front door. Two minutes more and she was in her car, still quietly talking to her reason for drawing breath, the man for whom she'd do anything.

"Harry, I miss you so much. Please, come back to me this time. I know it wasn't your fault they put your heart into that bitch instead of into a decent, strong male body like you need. I promise that with this next life, it will be different. And if not this next one, then the life after that or the one after that. I'll do this as many times as I have to in order to get you back with me. After all, true love doesn't give up. Isn't that what you always said?"

Reaper by James Pyles

"Come on, lover. Don't be shy. We've got the room for an hour. Let's have fun."

The money had already changed hands and Angel was lying on the bed with her blouse open and her jeans tossed on the floor.

"Can't say I'm shy, baby." He pulled off his shirt and got on top of her. He'd seen her on a street corner just off of Fremont Street and they settled on a price. She thought he was a dope because he didn't haggle, but then it wasn't just money that she wanted, and she certainly wasn't doing it for the sex.

"Just a little bit closer. Come on. I don't bite." She almost laughed because she was lying through her teeth.

"Oh I bet you do, but really, I don't mind."

He bent down to kiss her, which most of the hookers didn't allow, but in her case it didn't matter. She didn't care that he didn't use a condom either. Her eyes flickered, momentarily considering his throat. Might as well let him have his jollies first. No harm in it, she figured.

Then their lips met and she felt her throat tighten. Angel was paralyzed. The room began to swim and whirl. She tried to throw the john off her but her arms wouldn't move. What was he doing to her? What was that mist he was taking out of her?

As the last of her essence escaped Angel's body and nourished him, she began to shrivel, like a time-lapse film of aging and decay. In less than a minute, there was nothing left of the once beautiful and alluring young woman except a mummified corpse. She was his fifth victim that month, but they were getting more suspicious, so he'd have to move on to new hunting grounds soon.

Jack stood up wholly sated and put his shirt back on. Then he found her handbag, took his money back and then the rest of her cash. They had the room for another forty-five minutes but having finished with her, he was ready to leave.

The Las Vegas Review Journal would tag him the "Prostitute Killer," but while his victims worked the trade because it gave them a readily available food supply, he only stole the souls of the damned. Vampires were so convenient and cocky. They never realized that something stranger could be hunting them.

The Reaper walked back out into the night, thinking he might visit Los Angeles next.

Catering For The Hoard by Zoey Xolton

"Dinner for two? Menu item 354? Preparing in: Three—" says a welcoming, retail-friendly voice over the PA system.

Calvin stands bare and exposed at the centre of a shining metallic cell, cold and afraid. "So this is how it ends," he muses darkly.

"Two—"

He swallows hard. Digging deep he finds the last of his courage and turns to face the large, reflective glass panel. He knows they're watching…the bloody zombies.

"One—"

"Screw you, rotters!" he swears, saluting them with both his middle fingers.

"Initiate."

Jet-force blasts of air assault him from all sides, tearing and tenderising. The cell blossoms red as chunks of his flesh slide unceremoniously down the walls. Calvin collapses as merciful darkness claims him.

"Dinner is served. Enjoy."

The doors to the Feeding Booth slide open.

Eyes bulging, the undead couple salivate, licking their rotting maws in anticipation of their flesh-to-order Valentine's feast.

Heartbreaker by Terry Miller

Valentine's Day is a joke. Always has been, always will be. Kimberly knew this one would be no different. Flowers, cards, rings and the like are scattered across the hands of fools all intoxicated with endorphins that deceive the human mind. The thought that one could value another above the base carnality of desires is novel at best. We're all a number on a headboard chipping away at the sheetrock of the wall with each conquest. Love is a lie, lust an instinct; a reality.

Kimberly poured herself a shot of bourbon. She was a dark liquor girl to the core, fuck beer. The quicker the liquor, the quicker the not giving a shit. It was therapy and it served her well. The bar was quiet for a Tuesday but she figured it would pick up as the night wore on, all the singles gathering in hoping for a score on the big day of reminders of just how pathetic they are. Another shot, another inch to faded; Kimberly preferred the night a blur.

Ten o'clock and business was looking good. About two-thirds of the tables were full and the bar was loaded. Kimberly was more than happy to lend a hand in their pursuit of a one-night stand, that is, as long as they tipped well. Hell, she could use one herself.

A man at the end of the bar ordered a beer. "Whatever is on tap," he said. The glasses were chilled and the first half went down quick. He had obviously been pre-gaming before coming to the bar, his eyes just a bit glazed. Even so, he was far from falling over drunk. Kimberly gave him a smile. *Looks like a good victim*, she told herself.

"I know this is a little forward," the man said, "but what time to you get off?"

She looked at him for a moment. This was too easy. Through the years she came to appreciate *easy*.

"If I'm lucky, before you," she replied with a teasing wink.

He smiled and took another drink.

After the bar closed, the man waited patiently at the end for Kimberly to finish up. She disappeared in the back before returning with a change of clothes. She didn't want to venture outside soaked in a night's worth of spilled drinks. The man's pupils dilated as he drew her near him. She laughed and made no effort to fight. They kissed. Her heart began to race as she felt him stiffen against her. He drew away and peered into her eyes, a set of deep blues. His pupils narrowed. Her heart raced more. More. His eyes fixed on hers, he took her head in his hands as if to focus her gaze on him alone. Her chest hurt. Her tear ducts swelled and released as she fell to the floor. Her last breath exhaled in a puddle of tears. The man had gazed into her soul then broke her heart.

Mona Lisa Smile by Dawn DeBraal

Kevin hummed as he carved. Taking care in forming the lips into a sensuous curve. His creation was beautiful. Something he'd seen in his dreams, only now he was able to recreate his greatest wish: seeing the lovely Mona Lisa smiling at him. After all these years, that scowling face Mona Lisa had never graced him with a smile. Now that she was dead, he took advantage of this time. She would lay in her casket, and by God, she would be smiling at him, at everyone in the church.

His job as an undertaker and an artist was paying off.

Rose Garden by David Simms

Julie stared at the trail of rose petals that led from the front door to the bedroom. Maroon roses slept on the carpet to remind her. She had always wanted Greg to woo her with moments like this, but found through two years of hell, Valentine's Day ended up as Russian Roulette at best.

She assured that this year, romance would blossom, and flower, even if it wasn't his idea.

Where was he? She told him to be home by six.

Her ring still dazzled, diverting her eyes from the miasma of bruises on her forearm. Tonight, she would have her special night.

Greg had told her daily he loved her. Displaying that love hurt sometimes.

She recalled dropping the pieces, letting them fall, then nothing.

Tonight, only the holiday held the wounds of the relationship, wounds which she vowed would be healed by morning. Just yesterday, she felt her resolve shatter. An entity emerged that breathed its only breath, one that barely resembled the Julie she cursed in the mirror. The blaming she allowed often fucked away the fleeting confidence she flirted with every morning after.

He couldn't refuse her love tonight. Her therapist told her to take control of the situation and confront him, or leave. Julie hadn't told her the whole story, but both knew something burrowed within her, something that burned with a black fire.

Julie had squashed it for years. For too many guys.

When she began that morning, she mapped out the romantic plan for the evening. For hours, she toiled. Petals covered the beige carpet, staining it in an illogical pattern, trailing from where Greg would enter after his long day at work. Stains of flowers.

Did he already come home? Her head still buzzed from the fight.

She couldn't recall much after the spill of the first bouquet. A fist to the temple could cause memory loss, the doctors had told her.

On the bed, her mind whirred with fractured images, her body blossoming from the labors, the first positive pain she experienced in the relationship.

When would he return home?

Was that him whispering to her? He sounded close, yet weak.

The roses tainted the comforter in shades she smiled at, her tools strewn about.

Would Greg appreciate the effort? Would it finally soothe him? She needed peace to wash away the past, even what she couldn't recall from just hours ago.

The blows inflicted from bad days at work, ruined football games. They had effects. Compounding effects. Ones her therapists couldn't help with. Yet even they might smile a little at her efforts tonight.

With a twitch, she remembered that Greg had returned home earlier. The blades she dropped gleamed in the light, winked at her, a memory breaking through. A whimper sounded.

Greg rested now, beside the bed. She hoped he appreciated her efforts.

What was left of him, anyway.

Between the blank spots in her memories, one remained clear.

Romance wasn't dead. Not yet, anyway.

Worth It by Cassandra Angler

Sheila stood watching out the window from the darkened living room, her tight red dress clinging to her rounded belly. Drake sat in the car, looking at himself in the visor mirror as he tried to smooth out his disheveled hair. She left the window as he exited the car and lit the candles that she had placed on the dining room table.

"Wow," Drake said as he hung up his jacket. "Something smells amazing!"

"I wanted to surprise you," she said with a smile. "You've been working so much lately, I thought it would be nice to come home to a nice meal."

He said nothing, but smiled at her as he took his place at the table. She sat across from him, rubbing her belly as she ate. It only took Drake a few minutes to devour the steak and potatoes she had prepared. She stood and collected his empty dishes, dropped them into the sink and pulled a cake from the fridge.

Returning to the dining room, she placed the cake and a knife in front of her husband with a smile.

"Happy Valentine's Day, baby," she said cheerfully.

"Oh wow!' He slapped his hands together and cut the cake.

He placed a slice on the napkin in front of him and took a bite.

"Would you like me to cut you a slice?"

Sheila shook her head, her eyes never leaving the lipstick stain on Drake's neck. "Not right now, Love. Maybe later."

She sat back down and hummed to her pregnant belly as she watched him eat his slice of cake, even picking the crumbs up off the table with his fingertips and licking them clean.

"Good?" She asked.

"Amazing! You know peach is my favorite. A little grainy, but still really hit the spot."

He wiped his mouth with a napkin and stood to excuse himself. He stayed still, holding the edges of the table as the colour drained his face. Sheila smirked as Drake leaned over the side of the table and threw up. He wretched, lost his balance and fell to the floor, shaking.

Sheila stood and walked around the table, the smirk never leaving her face.

"I'm not as stupid as you think I am. I know where you go after work every night." She held her stomach as she drew her leg back and kicked Drake in the his.

He cried out in pain and tried to crawl away, his attempt making Sheila laugh. She walked around him and kicked him again. He rolled onto his back, looking up at her as bubbled bile spilled from the corners of his now blue lips, his eyes begging for mercy.

"I hope the little slut was worth it," she said, sitting in the chair beside him.

She crossed her legs and watched him struggle for oxygen. He stilled, hands collapsing to the floor beside him.

"Good riddance," she said before taking the car keys off the counter and heading for the door.

Love Always by Ximena Escobar

Love…was seeing him for the first time.

Love was the book he carried in his hand. His presence, like an imprint in the outskirts of my soul; the direction my smile went, and my eyes didn't.

Love was the songs he played, the sweater he wore. Waiting for the phone to ring, for hunger to pass and my jeans to fit.

Love was a knot in my throat, a hole in my stomach; digging my nails into his back and another's scratch marks out of my hands' reach.

But I did reach for the knife.

And that was love too.

Sweet Sacrifice by Eleanor Merry

"Do you truly love me, baby?" Luc asked, holding her chin to look up at him. She nodded eagerly.

"Oh yes, Master, I love you!" she exclaimed and Luc smiled, dropping his hand away.

"I know you do. And you want to make me happy, don't you baby?"

She nodded eagerly, glimmers of desire in her eyes. "Yes, Master."

He smiled again and walked across the room, letting his hands caress the tools spread across the table. Luc had been preparing and waiting for this moment for years and finally the day was here. It was February 14th, and his patience and hard work would finally pay off. A muffled scream let out behind him and he frowned, turning his attention to the other woman in the room.

He glowered at her but her eyes only got wider as she continued to shriek through the gag. Doing his best to ignore her, he turned back to his devout slave and gave her a warm smile.

"It's time baby," he told her, stepping away from the table to give her access. She smiled as she stood, making her way across the room. Her eyes lit up when she took in the table of implements and her breathing picked up.

"What would you like me to do, Master?"

Luc kissed her cheek and whispered into her ear, "Give me your pain."

She nodded and grinned as she took one of the knives off the table and Luc watched on with approval. Without hesitation she dragged the blade across the skin on her chest, moaning with pleasure as it cut through it like butter.

"Yes, baby, give me all your pain," Luc hissed, watching her. She brought the knife down to her nipple and looked up at him; his nod of approval was all she needed. Slicing down she removed one nipple, and then the second. The entire time she moaned in ecstasy, even when she brought the knife lower.

It had taken him a long time to turn her pain to pleasure, but the results were worth it. Luc got hard as he watched, entranced by this slave who would do anything for him. His willing sacrifice.

Piece by piece she cut and sliced, blood pouring to the floor until she was covered in red, still writhing in passion.

"Give it to me," he whispered and she smiled at him with love in her eyes before stabbing the knife into her own gut, crying out as orgasm overtook her even in her final breaths.

Luc sighed as he watched the life leave her before turning back to the other woman. Now for his unwilling sacrifice.

Soon, his Master would be free.

Devon, It's About The Details by Dawn DeBraal

She opened the card she found in Devon's drawer. There was a small box taped to it. He was finally going to ask her to get married. She was so excited. She carefully opened the box. Two karats, pear-shaped diamond. Nice! She then rewrapped the box and slid the card out of the envelope. It was going to be hard waiting for Valentine's Day when he asked her. The card read:

"Bernadette, be mine forever. I can't live without you! Devon." Her hand went to her mouth. Victoria couldn't believe it. Devon would get his wish: rat poison for supper.

Off-Menu by Joel R. Hunt

Arthur loved eating at *The Prancing Peacock.* He had bonded with the manager many years ago over their shared culinary tastes, and now he was allowed to order off-menu whenever he wanted. Even better, the *Peacock* offered a Valentine's Day special: two meals for the price of one. Arthur couldn't refuse.

He sat at his table and browsed the menu with leisure, looking for anything that might take his fancy. He was confident that he'd find something for his appetite. The *Peacock* always offered a varied selection. To start with, he ordered a bottle of wine and made himself comfortable, exchanging pleasantries with the familiar faces of the serving staff.

All night, couples drifted in and out. Some were barely more than children on their first dates, complete with sweat patches and compulsively checking of their phones. Others must have been celebrating marriages that spanned longer than Arthur's life. The couple just in front of him could have easily been his grandparents, but when they held hands over their wine, their eyes shone with a fiery youth. It was cute in its own way, Arthur had to admit, but it wasn't for him.

Instead, Arthur found his eyes lingering on a couple in the far corner. There was nothing exceptional or noteworthy about them; that was partly what attracted his attention. They seemed comfortable in one another's presence, but fell short of being affectionate. If it wasn't Valentines Day, they might have been mistaken for friends or siblings. The waiter brought a roast chicken dish for the man and a salad for the lady. Words were exchanged, the dishes were apologetically swapped, and Arthur quietly joined in as they laughed off the mistake. Nothing else of note happened between them, right up until they had finished their meals and asked for their bill.

As far as Arthur was concerned, they were the perfect couple.

His stomach rumbled, a reminder of the empty plate before him. Arthur smiled. Yes, it was time to order. He beckoned over one of the waiters who knew him and pointed across to the couple he had been watching.

"I'll have those two."

Burning Passion by Dawn DeBraal

Kevin wanted to be adventurous. Bernadette didn't want to, but agreed to handcuffs.

"But it's Valentine's Day!" Kevin made a big deal of cuffing her to the brass headboard. They both laughed because they'd been married for so long; this seemed kind of silly. Anything to spice things up. Suddenly Kevin clutched his heart. He fell forward, knocking the lit candle over. The fire started on the bedspread.

"Kevin!" Bernadette shouted, but Kevin was somewhere on the floor, unhearing. She tried to put the fire out with her knee, having no success, screaming when she saw flames climbing the wall.

Blah Blah Blah by Zachary C. Collier

He had killed her, in a sense, on a quiet snow dusted February morning in 1986 while she slumbered. He injected her with blood that carried the aids virus he had collected from a patient in his office that same day. She stirred but did not awaken. Weeks prior he discovered that she had been screwing some radiologist named Daniel and he refused to lose half of everything he had *earned* as a doctor in the divorce.

He had loved her and she had loved him too, despite her adultery. She used to ask him to dance with her in the shower while KC and The Sunshine Band played on, occasionally she'd wake him at night because stagnantly hot summer evenings turned her on and every Valentines day they had spent together she would take lipstick and write, "Roses are red, blah blah blah. I love you, Peter." And then she would place a kiss under the message with her plump lips. He had especially loved that.

Hatred *stems* from love. Love is the potent soil for which hate and jealousy and vile thoughts seem to bloom from. Hatred had brought him to an almost orgasmic joy when he had found that she had infected her lover. It was hatred that filled him like soured wine in a rusted cup when he had buried her and topped her grave with the cheapest headstone he could find. Thirty years later, however, it was fear he felt when the county sheriff showed up to inform him about her desecrated grave and her missing remains.

Days later a putrid stench invaded his home and Peter was awoken most nights by the sound of shuffling feet coming from downstairs. On February 13th he awoke to see all of the house plants, some of which Karen had cared for herself, were wilted brown and deceased. There were what appeared to be oddly shaped muddy footprints throughout his home and the convoluted path they weaved ended at his bedroom door.

"It's my house Karen!" He cried out in the stark silence. He inhaled deeply through his nose as if he enjoyed the carion odor that filled his nostrils. "I'm not going anywhere."

He attempted to sleep but her scent prevented it. Frustrated, he made his way to the already lit bathroom and that was when he saw it. Written in what appeared to be clay was Karen's Valentines Day message. The letters were thin and jagged as if written with the tip of a stone or a blunt pencil . . . or the bony end of a finger. Where her lip print should have been was a grayish brown smear with a tooth protruding from the muck. Peter felt his bladder quiver and warm urine filled the crotch of his pajamas. Not because of the message upon the mirror but because of the unmistakable sound of billowing bed sheets coming from his room. It sounded as if someone had just come home and crawled into bed.

Till Death Do Us Part by Danielle Sandidge

Tomorrow is Valentine's Day.

Five years ago tomorrow, we first laid eyes on one another.

Three years ago, in front of our family and friends, we vowed *"as long as we both shall live."*

How very special that we've been able to celebrate both. The world reminds us every year with aisles of hearts, balloons and chocolates that THIS is OUR time of year. This is OUR season.

I have been trying to come up with the best gifts, the ultimate Valentine's Day surprise. That's the only reason I even looked at your iPad. I wanted to see your searches on eBay.... I only wanted to look at your Amazon history. I wanted to browse your travel apps. A surprise weekend away?!?! Perfect! Best wifey ever award!

I can't believe you didn't have a passcode. Brad! What were you thinking? How can you be so bold? So assured? The pictures were not even in a hidden folder! I've never been so deflated and heartbroken in my life. I don't even know how to explain how I feel! I am humiliated. Saddened. Repulsed. DIRTY. I don't know if I should cry or scream or both.

The images. OH GOD, the images. They will be seared in my mind forever. For months, I have not been able to close my eyes without seeing those vile pictures.

Brad!!! Who ARE YOU?!?!? Brad, the man I love. The keeper of my stars. WHO are you?

At first, I thought it was a sick joke. Maybe you were just into sick true crime photos? I left it at that. Explained it away for just your love of the macabre, until the pictures from your business trip to Little Rock. Brad, she's just a little girl.

My heart broke time and again as I began searching missing girls in the cities you've been working in. Oh dear GOD, why!?! You?? The man that so gingerly held my hand as I was recovering from a migraine. The man that so tenderly nursed me when I got the flu. How can you be that sweet, loving man of mine? How can a beast exist in the same body that has so tenderly loved me in the gentlest of ways?

Never mind all of that now, Brad. I started planning our special event months ago. It was just after your parents left at Thanksgiving when I found those photos. I've had plenty of time to plan our special day. I worked so hard on this. A yurt in the mountains? The perfect romantic spot. Our dinner will put us to sleep forever, quietly slipping off to slumber as your soul is dragged to hell, Brad. I cannot live with myself. How could I have missed this? So many young girls will never grow old because I didn't see the monster beside me. You will NOT return to Little Rock for your next victim.

I intend to keep my promise, Brad. Till death do us part.

Payment by Scott Deegan

Janet stood watching as he reversed the car from her driveway, a brief stop as he shifted gears and then he was gone. Gone from her driveway, gone from her street, and gone from her life. The argument didn't leave with him, replaying over and over in her head and preventing sleep from finding her.

There were things she could have said to make him want to stay, but in the end she really didn't want him to. Her only regret was she could have said something more hurtful and crushed his precious ego. She was too nice for that. Instead she took the pain and ate it, allowing it to infect her and fester within.

She thought back to her parents and when they broke up. Their late night screaming fights, the long silent days when they hardly spoke to her let alone each other and how it ultimately ended with her mother in prison and her dad living out the rest of his days drooling on himself in a nursing home. She couldn't do something like that ever; repeatedly running someone over was not a thing she could manage.

Eric was a manipulative prick but he didn't deserve to be maimed by a speeding car. Well, at least most days he didn't deserve it. So Janet didn't even realize she was dreaming of revenge when she got the reading from the old fortune teller, but she listened when the elderly woman whispered in her ear.

Susan was Janet's BFF until she started sleeping with Eric and Janet felt more betrayed by Susan than she did by Eric. What the fortune teller said would have not leave either Susan or Eric untouched, both would suffer. Janet just had to pay the price and she wasn't sure she could bring herself to do that.

She loved her father; she still remembered the way he was and sometimes she imagined that he may return to that being that man. Those hopes were short lived however, the doctors never saying if those flickers of her Daddy that she saw were real, or just wishful thinking. To be honest, he was causing a great deal of distress on her finances and she wasn't sure how much longer she could afford this level of care. He would never dream of ending her care if the roles were reversed; he would do what it took to take care of his daughter. He endured a lot staying with her mother, but that was a different man than the one she'd known the last eight years. The man who sat in his own filth waiting for the nurses to clean him. The gypsy said her father had to die by her hand in order for the payment to be accepted, so when the doctor called and said he had a stroke Janet made her decision.

It was Wednesday morning when Janet picked up the pen with her hand, and signed the papers to end life support.

Love, Delivered by Chris Bannor

He loved her more than he could say. More than a thousand words could tell. More than any picture could show. He loved her with every cliché written. Every love song sung. Every poem ever penned. And so he spent hours making the perfect valentine.

In front of the whole third-grade class, she laughed. "Get away, Creep!"

He picked up the shredded valentine, and his heart, and carried them home. He grew. He learned. But he never loved again.

When the funeral was over, he placed the valentine on her grave. Maybe now, valentine delivered, he could finally love again.

It's A Love Story by Aindrila Roy

An off-key rendition of Taylor Swift's "Love Story" floated over to her. Below, the world rejoiced. Drunk on the most potent toxin of all, the singer was slowly swaying, holding her arms aloft. Love. It was in the very air, cloying and sickening in its sweetness, yet lethal when ingested. It doesn't kill its victim right away. It destroys, one sane thought at a time, till all is confetti.

Reva stood on the balcony, looking at the obscene display below and scrunched her nose in disgust. Love. *Pssh.* What a load of crock! Love had taken everything from her, leaving behind a husk.

Just then, the door to the apartment opened and he walked in. Draped on his arm was his newest arm-candy. Reva gritted her teeth and watched as Michael kicked the door behind him.

The two were locked by the lips while they undressed. Reva saw red. With a snarl, she walked up to the couple and yanked at the woman's hair. She screamed as her head jerked back. Blood dripped from her scalp as Reva continued to pull.

Michael's eyes widened as he looked around in evident panic. "Reva! Please, stop!"

"No. I will kill the bitch!"

"Please! Stop! Stop!" Michael dropped to his knees, begging. "Why are you doing this?"

With a grunt, Reva threw the woman aside, a little surprised that the latter almost flew to the table. A loud thud and the woman crumpled on the floor in a heap, unmoving. Michael screamed, holding his head in his hands.

"Why do you do this every time? Leave me alone!"

"Why?" Reva growled. "How dare you get these whores to our house while I am around."

It was as though she hadn't even spoken. Michael rushed over to the woman on the floor and checked her pulse. "She's alive. She's alive. Thank God!"

Reva gaped in disbelief while he pulled out her phone and dialed a number. Before the call could connect, however, she knocked the phone out of his hand. "Stop it!" he screamed. "Go away! I never loved you!"

With that, he picked the phone up and dialed again. Michael did not see Reva stumble back, as though hurt physically. Snatches of the past came back to her.

Valentine's Day.

A bouquet in her hand and love confession on her lips.

"I never loved you!"

Betrayal and heartbreak.

Her running to the balcony.

The feel of the air on her face as the ground reached to meet her.

"Hello!" Michael's voice drew her to the present. "My wife is hurt!"

Wife?

* * *

Reva stood in the balcony. Below her, the world celebrated the day of love. Just then, the door to the apartment opened and he walked in with his newest arm-candy draped on him.

Dinner Party by Angela Glover

Brian opened the door to a trail of red roses and lit candles leading to the aroma of a delicious meal in the kitchen.

As he rounded the corner to the dining room, an elegant spread was set but his smile faded at the sight of Amy sitting at the table with her back to him. He walked toward Amy, gasping in shock at the meal of her own heart and eyes along with a large platter of meat in the centre of the table.

Misty said, "Welcome home. We made you a hearty, home-cooked meal."

Startled, Brian turned around to face his wife as she approached him in black lace lingerie and heels, flashing her radiant smile.

"What have you done?"

Misty wrapped her arms around his shoulders and smiled. "What do you mean? We just wanted you to feel loved and appreciated."

Brian shoved her away, finally realizing that the platter of meat was Jane, Ava, Christine and Emma along with Amy. He screamed as the axe plunged into his chest, his last vision of his mistresses sitting in the living room covered in blood and his beautiful wife's smile.

"Happy Valentine's Day, dear!"

Margot, Mary, Lucy and Roger by DJ Elton

Women fall blindly in love with Roger and he uses each one for what's on offer, whether it's cash, sex, fun, travel, drugs, toys or gifts.

Mary is so thankful that Roger supports her doctor-shopping for the pain drugs that alleviate her regular existential agony. She has given Roger such attractive gifts over the past three years. He uses the car to impress his other women. The jewelry? The girls like it too.

"Darling, when you've stopped your little pill problem, then we'll get married. We need to be certain," he reassures Mary as they sit in a booth on their Valentine's dinner date.

"You're so practical." She smiles. A gorgeous face, with sad hollow eyes.

"I want us to be together, *soon*," she pouts, usually used to getting her own way.

Mary is glad that Roger's family live out of town because she feels anxious around people most of the time. Except with him. Such soft blue eyes and curly black hair, like a little boy. Oblivion brings bliss. But there is something not quite right about Roger; she just can't pinpoint it. Silly notion. She has another drink, telling herself not to be so sensitive.

Lucy met Roger in prison, where she was his psychologist. She understands his tormented, unfulfilled life. Her helpful codependent nature is stretched to the limit by this man, although it had initially seemed that he might be rehabilitated. Unfortunately that theory has lessened over the past five years. Lucy continues to have regular contact with him, even though she knows about how he treats his women, but she can't do much. She too is hopelessly in love with Roger because he is so charming, and attentive. Roger likes to overpower Lucy, and she submits to this power game. She can't deny her own neediness. Both are satisfied, but no-one is happy because they are both sick and living with lies. One day Lucy plans to leave this relationship because it hurts her physically and emotionally, but right now she isn't strong enough to do that.

Margot meets Roger at a breakfast café in the CBD, looking a little grey around the gills. They have met since the past six months. He thinks she's a diamond heiress, and she's a brilliant actress, playing the part so well. They're planning a trip to London together soon, and Roger is intrigued by Margot's stories of the celebrities to whom she will introduce him. He doesn't notice some of Margot's little habits. She's always texting, and taking shots on her cell phone, but Roger isn't concerned or suspicious about this. He thinks she's young and that's what millennials do. But Margot is a smart savvy girl with retribution in mind. Mary, Lucy and Margot all meet up regularly and are creating a foolproof plan. Margot has a spare basement where they will keep Roger, everyone will think he has gone to London. Both Mary and Lucy have a keen interest in pharmacology so that will keep him docile and pliant. Margot is going to punish Roger, bit by bit.

The Gift For Him by Trish McKee

Tyra took the young woman's hand and whispered, "Help a girl out. It'll be a fun night. Nothing too intense. I just want to give him a great Valentine's. Something a little more special than the usual dinner and dancing."

The woman, Corla, threw her head back and laughed. "You're the ultimate girlfriend. I would never let my boyfriend spend the evening with another woman."

Tyra lifted her shoulder. "What can I say? I adore him. I want to give him everything he wants."

It was what had brought her to this bar on Valentine's. She wanted to find a woman for Graham. As soon as she entered the bar, she had seen her. That tiny blonde sitting at the bar, sipping some colourful drink and staring around with huge, vulnerable eyes that shone like teary emeralds. She was easy to spot, her desperation soaking the air with its stench.

Convincing Corla had not been difficult. It never was, but this one had been particularly easy. She quickly confided to Tyra that her boyfriend of four years had left her, and she was lonely. She was sad. Everyone wanted love, but the recently heartbroken were especially vulnerable to that promise.

"Okay, can I see his picture?" She glanced at Tyra's phone and whistled. "That's him? Wow. Girl, if I were you, I'd be careful with sharing him. He's beautiful!"

"He is. So are you in?" Tyra was past the point of trying to explain her reasons. She did not need to. It was clear Corla was willing to do anything to soothe that screaming ache deep in her gut. Tyra knew it well. She understood the many ways one would try to silence it. To extinguish it.

Corla pretended to think it over. But then she nodded. "I'll go. But I just want to meet him. See how everything goes. I just…I'm not one for one-night stands. This is a little out of my comfort range."

"Of course," Tyra cooed. "Your pace. We can just have a fun evening talking and drinking."

Once at the house, she led Corla to the back room of the basement.

"Graham," she sang out, opening the door and gently pushing Corla inside. Graham was slumped over, his glowing yellow eyes rising to meet hers, his fangs glistening, drool dripping from the corner of his mouth almost immediately. "Happy Valentine's Day, my love. I brought you dinner."

Tyra tried to look away before she caught that look of terror. She did not get pleasure from this part of it. She merely wanted to feed her love so that he was the Graham she knew and adored. This was a necessity. But she caught the paling of the young woman's face, the scream piercing the air as she turned to flee. But Graham's reflexes were extraordinary, and he swooped over her before she could even step toward the door. And he drained her blood before Tyra could even explain how she had met her.

Swipe by Natasha Sinclair

I'm not too fond of Valentine's Day. Card store love on steroids. It's bullshit.

Mine has become somewhat of an annual ritual. This year, I want to better the last, aiming for a personal best—a city break with souvenirs.

My aim is six in one night. I can take it, I'm an experienced woman, and I know my limits. Tinder is my menu, an array of tasty tapas, and they always swipe—"Hot busty brunette, strictly no strings attached SEX." And it's true; I am hot, and I'm looking for his detachment.

I'll swipe and ride. Always at his place, and he must live alone.

"How high can the volume go on your stereo? This might get out of control."

Volume up to cover the screams.

I move in, lust in the lead, testing out the merchandise; must feel it inside, alive and pumping with as much power as it's ever going to have. Afterwards, as he comes down sweaty and breathless from the fuck of his life, I give him what appears to be a thank you suck. Taking it slow and sloppy to start, a good old "oh I can't get enough of your wonderful cock" suck, and that's true too; I can't.

I'll go down, and it's the same every time as I let my flowing hair and soft hands caress his sweaty thighs, with my mouth licking and sucking until he starts to stiffen again. I feel the pulse through him, it tickles my tongue, and I resist the urge to bite down—what a waste that would be with such horrid ragged edges.

They never see the blade coming; eyes closed in false, fleeting security.

Slicing from the base of his shaft against his balls towards his belly. The meat is tough, but my blade is smooth, as am I. They always spurt so vigorously; sweet, angry red from those fired up protruding veins. It gets in my hair, sprays in my mouth, hot fast metal, painting my skin crimson spatters. This is my favourite part; I come every time, harder the louder they scream; a symphony. Collapsing in ecstasy with my new souvenir in hand, trusty blade in the other.

A quick shower and clean up while stud number one is passed out from blood loss. My new memento in the bag. "Happy Valentine's, baby."

Only 10:30 pm, plenty of time. One down, five to go.

Onto Tinder, *Mmm, you'll do...*Swipe.

Patient X by Nico Bell

Cameron's hand trembled as she pressed the scalpel against the patient's chest. Sweat beaded her brow as she narrowed her eyes, focusing on the incision.

Dr. Shiflette sucked in a breath. "Careful, darling. Keep the slice clean and crisp."

Cameron chewed her lower lip and refocused.

Open the chest cavity.

Cut the sternum.

Proceed with the extraction.

The patient's screams went unanswered as his wrists strained against the restraints.

"Oh dear." Dr. Shiflette sighed and stroked the man's forehead. "Perhaps he's regretting breaking all those hearts. What do you think, Cameron? Should we stop now? Stitch him up? Risk sending him back into the world?"

Cameron looked at the dark blood of his chest and thought of her sister. Her beautiful older sister who trusted this man, loved this man, gave four years of her life to this man.

And he cheated.

Lied.

Tossed her aside on Valentine's Day.

Cameron rolled back her shoulders. "No, we'll continue. I really appreciate your help, ma'am."

"Of course. Us ladies need to stick together."

"Good." Cameron set aside the scalpel and picked up the bone saw. "Then let's cut out his heart."

The Perfect Valentine by Nicole Henning

The restaurant was packed, the line around the building. Everyone seemed to want to show their love by purchasing ridiculously overpriced plates of snack portion-sized food. She sat at her table waiting with a bored expression on her face, her pale blonde hair piled on the top of her head and her ruby red dress hugging her curves. Her water had been refilled three times already and she was beginning to think her date had stood her up. Right when she was going to give up and leave, he sauntered over to the table and sat down.

She smiled and accepted the single rose he presented her with and blushed as a waiter rushed over with a single stem vase for her. He ran a hand through his perfectly slicked back hair and droned on and on about his hobbies and interests. She smiled and nodded when required but didn't add much to the conversation. She knew everything she needed to already thanks to his dating site profile. He was full enough of himself that it didn't faze him when she didn't divulge personal information. They ate and he drank whiskey on the rocks while she sipped demurely on a glass of white wine. When he got up to go to the bathroom, she ordered him another whiskey and was swirling it with her pointer finger when he came back. She slipped the finger between his lips and let him suck it before giving him a grin and downing the rest of her wine. He followed with his whiskey and paid the check before escorting her to her car.

She drove while his hand moved up her thigh slowly. Swatting at his hand she licked her lips and gave the promise of *soon*. When they pull into her garage, he clumsily tried to grab her and she laughed before bolting and running away, leading him through her house while she taking off her clothes

THE PERFECT VALENTINE BY NICOLE HENNING

one piece at a time. He drunkenly followed after her until he fell to his knees in the living room, plastic sheeting crinkling under him as he crawled.

The room spins and he looked up questioningly.

The drug she had slipped into his last glass of whiskey had rendered him defenseless.

She almost felt sorry for him, but remembered how much she wanted to please her love with the gift of this selfish man. She stood naked over him and smiled as her love walked into the room, naked and ravenous. The She-Demon's cracked blackened skin glistened in the light of the black candles placed around the room. She pounced on the man and feasted on his flesh until he was nothing but bones. When she stood and embraced her human, they made love with his blood slickening their bodies. They both moaned and writhed against each other as their passion mounted. The She-Demon purred in satisfaction as she took in the carnage and her orgasming lover.

It was a perfect Valentine's Day.

He Lusted For Me by Andrea Allison

"You're sight belongs to me," Lady Margaret said, eyeballs slipping from her fingers.

"Please. I've done nothing wrong," the girl sobbed.

"You stole my son's heart away from his beloved and you say you've done nothing wrong. You're schemes must come to an end."

"He lusted after me!"

"Silence! My son will marry on the day of love and we will have the life the witch promised." She ran the blade along the girl's skin as she screamed. "You will remain strapped to this table. The rats will have their way with you. Pray for warts in your next life."

The Colour of Trauma Healing by Natasha Sinclair

As a child, she lost the tip of her pinky, from that top knuckle up. That's what sparked the allure. The healing of that little stump was magically mesmerising - the pain over time dulling to a stinging itch, then numbness to a phantom tip. The colour changes, through a spectrum of greens, purples, blues, yellows, reds and pinks; the colour of trauma healing.

That's what Trish needed now—a visual measure after heartbreak. That organ wasn't exactly something she could remove; a little toe was more realistic. *Nothing to miss there really, it's practically a stump as it is, an ugly residual little thing,* she thought.

Glancing up at the calendar, 14th of February, it was a few months yet until summer, ample time to "heal." An open toe shoe never reveals the little one anyway.

Trish fetched the pink-handled pruning shears from beneath the kitchen sink. This set was brand new. She bought two sets last summer, one for her rose bushes beneath the front window in the garden, and one should she require some pruning herself. The curve of the blade seemed perfect for small digit amputation. Every time she pruned a bush, the strong curve of those blades flirted with her; a little amputation could be as effective for her as it was her roses that bloomed and grew all the better for their loss.

While drawing a hot bath she washed and sterilised the shears. Lavender tea lights adorned the bathroom sill. She poured a large glass of Rosé, and set it on a small table beside the tub along with her favourite dark chocolate box— a holiday treat for one as the last of the day's light receded into the frigid evening.

While she steeped in the bath, her shears now sat beside the other treats by the tub. She wiggled her toes just at the edge of the surface of the bubbles. It didn't even wiggle, the smallest, her foot runt—such a useless little thing. Pulling her foot up with her hand she dug her perfectly manicured nails into the little toe and barely felt it.

After a large gulp of wine, she swiftly swapped the glass for the shears, pulled her foot up again with her other hand and cut down hard. A searing agony shot through her foot and entire right leg; flashes of incandescent lighting bolting through her bones. Gritting her teeth so tight her jaw crunched (in unison with her toe) she sucked hot damp air in through her teeth. The little pink toe plopped off into the romantically crimson blood-spattered bubbles. Blood spurted from the raw stump, the flesh around it flopped a little around the bone. More beautiful than she imagined.

When You Put It That Way by Galina Trefil

"Do you remember what you said to me one year ago today?" Darla demanded as Robert slid the jewelry box across the table towards her. Between them, candles, the room's only light, flickered romantically. Robert raised his eyebrows, shrugging, as he poured them both a glass of champagne. "I said that I was tired of being your mistress!" she snapped.

"Oh, that." His tone was maddeningly casual.

"Yes, *that!* And you promised me that you would marry me!"

"And?"

"Well," she scoffed, "we're not married, are we?"

He leaned forward, interlocking his fingers before his face. "Why do you play these games with me?" She scowled. "You know what I could do to you. You know that if I go to the press or IRS…or the police…."

"You'd never do that."

"Why shouldn't I? You've hardly made it worth my while to keep my mouth shut. Look at me. I'm young. I'm beautiful. These are the best years of my life. This is when I need to ensure my future. If you're not serious about committing to me long-term, why should I waste any more time on you? And why shouldn't I punish you for making me spend three goddamn years in limbo? You've gotten what you've wanted, Robert. Now it's time for me to get mine."

"Open your present."

"You think that I'm joking?" She shrieked. "After all this time of me being your secretary, I have enough data to destroy that company of yours. And, after the government liquidates all of its and your personal assets, you'll wind up in prison, taking it up the tailpipe all day long! And I'll do it too if you don't—"

"Don't give you an engagement ring, like the one that's right there in that box right now?"

She gaped. Glee exploded across her face. She forgot all of her threats, ripping the box open, and slamming the massive clump of diamonds down over her finger. "Oh, Robert!" She beamed. "We're going to be together forever and ever now!"

"Till death do us part, baby."

"I didn't think that you wanted to be with me anymore."

"Silly girl. How could I ever let a gem like you go?"

As she began babbling incessantly about how much she loved him, Robert smirked. No, no, he wouldn't be losing the company that he'd worked hard to build. And, so long as her body was never found, he wouldn't be going to prison either. Only she knew about all of the illegal things that he'd done to get his business off of the ground and now, soon, all of that information would die with her.

"Engaged on national day of love," she sighed, enraptured by the sight of so many glistening carats. "What could be sweeter than that?"

A ring covered in cyanide, my darling, he mused. Learning back in his chair, he sipped at his champagne with a sense of victory, ready to savor every moment of what came next.

Pierced by M Ennenbach

She glared at me across the crowded restaurant. I glared right back. Who does she think she is? I've never seen her before. Couldn't pick her out of a lineup. Yet there she stands, glaring at me with eyes filled with hate.

Then everything in the room changed. In an instant, her hatred was forgotten.

As I watched her watching me, I saw a blur speed through the air. My jaw dropped as she clutched her chest. What in the fuck was that sticking out of her chest? It looked like an arrow. Impossible. She looked down in shock at it for a moment then back at me. Now her expression was decidedly different.

I blinked at the feathered shaft, watched as blood spread across her white button down shirt. I couldn't fathom what was happening. And her eyes never left mine. She never moved except to clutch the offending arrow. Then she smiled demurely and blew me a kiss.

It was at that moment I saw the little bastard in a diaper zipping through the room. Watched as he let loose a volley from his small golden bow. I felt my pulse race as the woman across the room began to maneuver towards me. I backed away, bumping into people around me. Then the imp caught my eye, a devilish grin on his cherubic face. He reached slowly to the quiver on his side and sighted down the shaft at me.

I let out a small cry and dove towards the ground. My sudden movement caused chaos around me. In my fall I pulled an angry looking man in front of me and watched as an arrow planted itself in his throat, right beneath his Adam's apple. He let out a gurgling cry and fell along with me.

I scurried across the floor, head on a swivel as I looked for the flying bastard and his accursed arrows. I could see nothing but legs and frightened faces looking down at me. Then I crawled into a set of shapely legs. I fearfully followed them up and met the eyes of the once hateful visage from across the room. I tried to cry out as I felt a sudden pain in the left buttock.

Then I slowly got to my feet and took the hand of this ravishing creature. How did I not see how beautiful she was? The distance between must have cast an illusion. There was no way a woman as spectacularly gorgeous could ever give a look less than that of home. And I could tell, with no doubt whatsoever, she was mine.

Out of the corner of my eye, I saw a shadow flit amongst the crowd. I did my best to ignore it. I had a vision in front of me that was more than enough to fill my gaze for the rest of my life. Even as I heard a small voice in the back of my skull screaming. One easily forgotten.

Fevered by Cassandra Angler

The fever set in, the bite mark on his side throbbing as Joel walked. A bouquet of flowers grasped in his hand, picked by hand along the way.

Just a few more feet, he told himself. The grave marker was already in view between the trees. He heard the screams of the contaminated in the distance, the call of a meal being spotted. The smell of rotten flesh thick in the air.

He kneeled and laid the flowers beside the wooden cross and sighed. Even after three years, it still hurt. Especially today. Her name written beautifully across the wood in cursive marker, faded by rainwater and time, tugged at his heart.

"I think this is it, Willow," Joel said, slumping down against a tree. "A little one took a chunk out of me. I couldn't bring myself to shoot it."

He pulled his pistol from the waistband of his jeans and laid it in the grass beside him. "I left the kids with the group. They'll be well taken care of."

A bolt of pain shot up his side, the bite mark, bleeding down his side, throbbing with his pulse. "At least this will be the last Valentine's Day we have to be apart, my love."

Joel leaned forward, placing the flowers against the wooden cross, watching as they fanned out. His vision started to blur, a wet streak running down his cheek. He touched his face and sighed at the sight of blood on his fingertips. His hands had already started to discolour, the veins swelling underneath swelling.

"I made it in time, Darling. Though I didn't think I would. I am so weak. My only regret is that I won't be able to bury myself here, next to you."

Joel lifted his pistol, pressing the barrel against his temple. His hands trembled beneath its weight.

"I'm coming baby," he said and pulled the trigger.

Click.

Joel looked at the gun confused and pulled out the magazine, finding it empty.

"No," Joel breathed, voice trembling. "This can't be happening."

The sound of twigs snapping somewhere in the woods broke through his despair. He threw his head back and released an anguished scream. He heard footsteps approaching, heavy thumping against the earth as they closed in.

They broke through the tree line baring their teeth in a hungry sneer, bloody foam seeping from the corners of their mouths.

"Right here, asshole!" Joel yelled.

A chorus of screams filled the air as the herd pounced on him, their teeth and fingers prying the flesh from his bones.

"Happy Valentine's Day, baby," he gurgled thought the blood spilling from his mouth, his vision fading to black.

The Indoctrination by Daileas Duclo

"Settle down everyone, I know y'all are excited and our time is near," the tall man spoke reproachfully. Everyone listened. They had been waiting for this day, Valentine's Day. The time of their ascension was here. The tall man called himself Jilt and everyone here hung on his every word like gospel.

"I know the people out there have wronged you and they abandoned us, but I will never abandon you," Jilt spoke. They listened. "Today is our reckoning. All the people in that supermarket are buying and taking for their special someone," he said with malice in his voice.

"They consume and they take because of what they believe they will receive in return, love or lust. They can't tell the difference," Jilt shook his head disapprovingly. "Today we'll show them the true love!" The crowd cheered, fanatically waving objects that gave off a glimmer of refracted light high above their heads.

"Yes, yes we will," Jilt responded. The doors to the supermarket opened and shut like any automated doors did and people filed in and out, oblivious to the crowd of strange purple-robed figures in the sprawling parking lot. They were too occupied with rushing home to their loved ones to bring them candy, light candles or prepare that nice dinner they promised. Pity; none of them were going to make it.

"Reach out, reach out and touch someone," Jilt chanted maniacally, and his followers did. They rushed through the parking lot and through the doors of the supermarket stabbing indiscriminately. The blood pooled in the parking lot and people died.

The Commune of the Wounded Heart had been unleashed and they were ready to share their love with the world.

Where The Blame Lies by Galina Trefil

"After we were married, it didn't take me long to realize that Henry would always prefer Clara to me," Sadie remarked bitterly inside the jail to her lawyer. "Oh, sure, everyone takes it for granted that a man will never completely lose it for his true 'first love,' but on our wedding day, I thought that he loved me best. Soon I learned that I was nothing to Henry but a convenience—a cook, a maid, a sex toy. An extra paycheck. Clara was the one who really mattered to him."

"Do you feel any remorse?"

"For committing murder? No, not at all. Why should I?"

"Most people would feel regret."

"Look, I'll fake it in court. I don't mind sobbing on the witness stand. But am I actually sorry? Hell no. They shared a terrible secret and forced me to live with it. They brought a good murdering on themselves."

The lawyer swallowed uneasily. He'd defended plenty of killers, but most of them were hardened criminals. This young woman, who still had the fresh-faced appearance of a high school teenager, had not so much as a parking ticket to her name. And the story she told…. What she'd done to the body….

"The flowers that were laid over the corpse—"

"Valentine's Day," she cut him off. "Given that we had a lover's triangle, I thought a bouquet was appropriate. It seemed…festive."

"And was it 'festive' to mix Clara's blood into frosting?"

"Ah, so the investigators found out about that, did they?" Sadie smirked.

"How do you plan to explain it to the jury?"

"I will say that I baked my husband a heart-shaped cake, filled with his lover's heart and topped with her blood. And then, as they sit there gaping at me, horrified as can be, I will add that Clara still had it coming to her," Sadie chuckled. "So did Henry."

"Are you disappointed that, after Henry ate the heart, he survived the stabbing that you gave him?"

"At least the two of them aren't united in death," she shrugged.

"Tell me: why were you so jealous of Clara? What did you see or hear that would make you think that their relationship was inappropriate?"

"A wife knows when her husband's in messing around with another woman," she scowled. "Especially if the other woman lives right next door, it becomes impossible, try as one might, not to notice what's happening." Sadie glared, knowing what he was thinking. Clara had just been a sweet, middle-aged lady. She'd sung in the church choir, had been known for her charitable work in the community. "They had a very dark relationship," Sadie spat defensively. "Otherwise, I wouldn't have killed her."

"But she wasn't some random girlfriend. She was—"

"His mother, yes! Exactly! And that's why I had to stab her and why I'd do it again!" Clara snapped. "You think that I'm sick, but I'm not half as sick as they were. I told you: they had it coming."

My Angel by Scott Deegan

Seven years ago

I met her in junior high, the seventh grade to be exact. My Angel.

My dad had been drinking that night, and when he drank he got violent. He backhanded me across the nose and shoved me into the wood stove, burning the side of my face. When Mom tried to intervene, he shifted his focus and his rage towards her. That's when I ran. I hated leaving her but I was only twelve. What could I do? I had been running for quite a while when the stitch in my side and the pain of the burn became too much and I collapsed on the ground, sobbing. When I looked up she was standing above me.

The moon hung full behind her, framing her in its magnificent light and reflecting off her halo. She stared down at me with more love in her eyes than I ever felt in the entirety of my life. I had never seen anything more beautiful than her. Her perfect porcelain skin, her magnificent wings spread out behind her, and her copper halo brought a peace to me I've never known. I professed my love for her then and there.

I would visit her often after that night, telling her my feelings, my hopes, my dreams, and my fears. She never spoke to me but she never turned away from me either, not like my family did. I was always safe with her. I'd never had that feeling.

My family found out and tried keeping us apart but I would find a way to see her. I would sneak out in the middle of the night, it got so bad the police brought my home several times. Finally, my parents sent me to a home for runaways to keep me from my Angel.

Release Day

The doctors told me my Angel isn't real and that I need to focus on the world around me. At first I fought this, asked them what was so good about my world that it deserved my attention. As the years went by I learned their system of rewards for desired performance. So I quit trying to leave the hospital and I performed, but I never forgot my Angel. How can you forget the one that saved you?

So now I'm back in the town where I spent the first part of my life and nothing is the same. My father is gone, run off to who knows where, and my mother is a broken person. Broken by my father's abuse and the stigma of having a crazy child. The people here watch me constantly, always looking always judging. It's all too much. I only have one person to talk to.

My Angel still stands in the same place but like me she has been affected by the years. Her skin is now pot-marked, her wings broken, and her copper halo is tarnished. Her flaws make her beautiful and I love her more. My Angel, the guardian standing on the hill of St. Mary's cemetery.

Candy Hearts by Nicole Henning

Valentine's Day: the words conjure images of love and affection. But what is the reality of V-Day? People buy flowers and sweets to suck up for being abusive or neglectful the rest of the year. A box of chocolates and roses don't make up for poor treatment. You need to appreciate every moment you have with someone. If you take them for granted, well, you deserve what can happen to you. I stood leaning against the brick wall outside the grocery store when I overheard one side of a conversation.

He was walking towards me talking loudly on his cell phone earpiece while texting. I got out my phone and pretended to not pay attention to him. His voice was loud as he continued to talk and text.

"I know baby, I need to spend some time with her. I know it doesn't seem fair, but she is my wife! I'm texting with her right now; she's been emotional lately. I will not break up with my wife on Valentine's Day. We can go out tomorrow night. Damn, she needs to call me. I'll talk to you later."

Tapping his earpiece, he pocketed his phone and walked into the store and said, "Hello. What do we need?"

I followed him through the store as he picked up things here and there. A pineapple, lunch meat, and potatoes went into his basket along with a bouquet of long-stem roses and a bag of candy hearts.

I followed him home. He drove a little over the speed limit and talked animatedly over speaker phone. He pulled into his driveway, checked himself out in the rearview mirror and he ended his phone call. By this time, I was already in his house. Waiting upstairs I shifted from foot to foot. I stood behind the bedroom door. After five minutes he came upstairs. He opened the door and dropped the open bag of candy on the floor.

He saw his wife tied to the bed, stiff rope biting into her wrists and ankles. A scarf wrapped around her head gagging her. He stood next to the bed in shock. I came out from behind the door and used the large kitchen knife I had taken from the butcher block downstairs to cut his throat. After he was dead, I climbed onto the bed and straddled his wife. Smiling I removed her gag and leaned down to give her a kiss. Our tongues probed each other's mouths.

I freed her wrists and let her go to work on her ankles while I got his phone from his pocket. Texting his mistress, saying he needed her and that his wife had left him. I smiled, thinking of her horrified face when she would find him dead on the bedroom floor. Once my love was unbound we put the rope in her bag and left the bedroom, stepping on the spilled candy hearts as we went.

Family Dinner by Trish McKee

Vicki smiled at Mason and felt a ripple of irritation when his lips wobbled in a weak response. Fortunately, it simply appeared as if he was nervous. And why shouldn't he be? He was spending Valentine's Day at her parents' house, meeting her family for the first time.

"So Mason, how did you two meet?" Sally, Vicki's older sister asked, her own grin flirtatious.

He stared at her dumbfounded for a moment before answering. "Oh. We…met at a gas station. It was like being knocked on the head."

Laughing, Vicki elaborated, "He just stood there and didn't know what to say. It took forever to convince him we should go out. He's shy."

Vicki's mom guffawed. "Having to convince a man to go out with you. That's embarrassing."

Sally grinned. "I never had to convince anyone."

"Well, when you offer everything up front, I guess not," Vicki quipped, narrowing her eyes.

The dinner was painstakingly long. At one point, Vicki had to nudge Mason and remind him to eat. He merely nodded and slowly chewed, his gaze on his plate.

Finally they made their exit. She was pleased to see Mason ignore Sally's attempts to get close to him, instead his focus entirely on her, watching to see her moves, mirroring her steps. It appeared as if he were smitten. She knew her parents were impressed.

Once in the car, he asked her what was next.

" Just sit back and enjoy the ride," she laughed, but he merely stared out the window.

Then he turned to her. "Why didn't you just hire someone to be your date at this dinner?"

"Did that before. Caught the guy making out with Sally at the end of the night."

"Oh. Shit. What happened after that?"

Vicki took her eyes off the road to stare him straight in the eyes and answered, "He went missing."

Mason sat back, sweat glistening at his temples.

And as if not noticing his sudden discomfort, she continued talking, "It's ridiculous. A family dinner on Valentine's. But if I go without a date, I'm a disgrace." She paused and then snapped, "Are you listening?" Before he could answer, she pulled onto a narrow dirt path.

"Here?" He looked around. "Our car—"

"You want to survive?" She tapped her waistline where her gun was hidden.

He quickly nodded and followed her as she got out and opened the trunk.

"Oh my God, Mary." He bent forward, grabbing the woman that was tied up and gagged. "Are you okay?"

"She's gone," Vicki informed him evenly. "Gave her something that was quick and painless. I figured once you went to dinner with me, you wouldn't want her." When he started wailing, she rolled her eyes. "Listen, you gonna help me get rid of the body or what? We can go out for dessert afterwards. It's still early." And once again, she tapped where her gun was hidden. "It's Valentine's Day."

Man in the Mirror by Lea Vida Del Moro

"People say that if you wish with all the sincerity of your heart in front of the mirror, you will see the man of your dreams."

It is a fairy tale that many young women have heard, and I, for one, look forward to testing it out on my own fantasy man.

Really, I wish that I could be like my mother. Her first and last love was my father. It's not an easy thing to follow, but maybe that is part of the mystery of love.

So here I am in front of the mirror holding a candle, chanting a spell with my little cousin Lorie.

"Mirror mirror on the wall…show me who's the lucky guy destined for me forever…."

I continue to repeat the spell again and again, until I feel something happen.

The room is suddenly filled with a cold breeze; the fog coming from nowhere. My cousin Lorie screams as a strong wind carries her away.

"Lorie? LORIE!" I grip with her hand but she slips until she is pulled away and nowhere to be seen in the fog. I run, calling out her name, but she doesn't respond. I think I am alone in the room until someone whispers.

"Who's there?" I ask fearfully as I look around. I see a shadow inside the mirror. I step closer and the shadow creates a figure. A man with two horns. His eyes blazing and ferocious with long tail that twists and weaves behind him.

I scream as I take it in. The Devil in the mirror. Lorie is gone. The man of my dreams…. My fright overwhelms me and I collapse, falling to the ground.

A few minutes pass before I open my eyes. I look up and see someone else in front of me. A man dressed in a white polo shirt and black trousers. He is handsome and looks young. He smiles at me and takes my hand. I'm confused at first, but then my fear melts away and I feel my heart beat fast as I take his hand. We dance through a waltz, the music weaving its way into my heart and soul. The room is filled with the brightness and fire of the sun.

My happiness overflows as his lips meet mine and I'm a goner. I close my eyes and cherish the moment....

"Margarette, wake up! It's getting late!" Lorie shakes me and I wake up in a daze.

"How was your Valentine's Day? And where did you get that ring from? Do you have a boyfriend?" she asks as I begin to wake from the strange dream.

I look down and see the ring on my left hand. Smiling to myself, I begin to hum as I run my hands over the ring.

Devil or Prince Charming? Either way, he's mine.

The Reunion by Daileas Duclo

It had been five years since she left him. No, five years since that drunk driver stole her from him forever.

Every Saturday night, Martin came to the graveyard to visit her and mourn his losses. At first her relatives and their friends would accompany him to the site to remember her and pay tribute to her. Those days had passed and now Martin came here alone, and if he were honest with himself, he preferred it that way. No one knew his Tabitha the way he knew her.

That was all over now, though. He finally found that driver and bound him. He rushed to the graveyard with the dusty old book and candles like the woman said. This ritual would bring them together. All he had to do is make sure to chant the words clearly and remember not to miss when he plunged the knife into that bastard's heart.

"Comte bacto memorium," he chanted and then drove the dagger home. Everything had a cost, but he would pay any price to get Tabitha back.

"Darling, you've returned," he exclaimed as Tabitha rose from her crypt still wearing the wedding dress she was buried in, the vitality streaming over her.

"Do you love me?" she asked, eyes glimmering with tears.

"Yes!" he exclaimed. She eyed him and said, "Then you must bring me more of them." She gestured to the body of the driver and then began to feed.

Family Traditions by Andrew Kurtz

My name is Jack Riper. If this bears any resemblance to Jack the Ripper, you are not far from the truth.

My parents, Joseph and Fran Riper, were fascinated by serial killers and their favorite was Jack the Ripper. In addition to being fascinated, my parents were actual serial killers and cannibals.

Thirty years ago, on Valentine's Day, my parents abducted a young man and woman from off the street. The young couple was shopping for Valentine's Day gifts when they were kidnapped.

The helpless victims were brought to the cellar of our house, which was equipped with a multitude of tools.

Both victims were stripped nude and tied to chairs with heavy rope.

My father chopped the young man's hands off with an axe. Blood poured onto the cold concrete floor from the gaping wound, creating a sanguine pool. Afterward, he gouged out the man's left eye with a screwdriver and forced the eye down the man's throat. My father just laughed and urinated in the man's mouth. The man's screams became gurgles. The urine had such a foul stench that I almost vomited.

When my father castrated the man's phallus with a chainsaw, I vomited. Blood gushed from the man's groin area. My father held the man's penis in his hand, dipped it in the blood, and masticated it slowly in his mouth. He gave a loud burp and licked his bloodstained lips with his tongue.

When he cracked the man's head open with a sledgehammer, it reminded me of an egg breaking. The man's brain flopped onto the ground, followed by its owner.

My mother snipped off the young woman's nipples with a scissor, making her cry out in agony. Afterward, my mother utilized a long sharp kitchen knife and disemboweled the woman. All of the internal organs slowly poured out. Upon recovering the woman's still-beating heart, my mother mutilated it. The mutilated organ was handed to my father, who ate it.

My father used a power drill to open the man's chest and remove his heart too.

He gave it to my mother and wished her a happy Valentine's Day. My mother was overjoyed and devoured it.

Today is Valentine's Day, 30 years later. My parents have been dead for many years, but I still observe our Valentine's Day traditions.

You must excuse me. I have a young couple in the basement who require my attention.

The Things He Did For His Wife by Chris Bannor

He never understood Valentine's Day. He spent every day of his life showing his wife just how much he loved her. She was his everything. Still, he faithfully had roses sent to her work (to make her coworkers envious) and sent lilacs to their home (her favorite). He had chocolates in hand and a good bottle of wine chilling.

Later, when she was asleep, he'd slink down to the garage for his own games. The couple in the trunk would learn that they should never have been so disrespectful as to have a lover's spat on his wife's favorite holiday.

Safe Sex by Galina Trefil

Bob sat at the bar, waiting, knowing that he wouldn't have to wait too long. Given that Valentine's Day was in twenty-four hours, every creep in the room tonight could only be thinking about one thing: getting laid. And it was a fact known to many of them that Bob was the guy who could make sure that happened.

A squirrelly youth, probably a college kid, sat next to Bob. He wore a winter trapper hat, complete with bulky, concealing ear flaps. For a minute or two, he kept anxiously looking over his shoulder. A new customer. Bob waited for him to work up the nerve to speak. "Hey," he finally murmured, not looking at Bob. "I hear that you're the guy who helps people out in the romance department." Bob sipped his beer, smirking, but didn't respond. "If you've got something to sell—a love bug, I mean—"

"A love bug?" Bob chuckled. Geesh, why couldn't these idiots ever just come right out and say it?

"An aphrodisiac."

"GHB, my young friend," Bob laughed. "Is that what you want?"

"Yeah." He pulled out his wallet, filled with a generous wad of cash, and flashed it briefly. "I've only got three hundred on me. Is that enough?"

Yeah, that was enough—more than enough. Bob grinned, realizing that he'd be sold out of product for the night. "That'll do," he nodded, trying to retain his composure.

"I don't want anyone to see us make the exchange," the kid told him, adjusting his hat flaps nervously. "Meet me in the parking lot in five minutes."

Bob did as instructed.

In the darkness, walking towards the kid's pickup truck, he never saw the blow coming. An hour later, lying face down in the dirt in the woods, Bob found himself blinking as blood trickled down from a wound on his temple into his eye. Gradually, he realized that he was gagged and bound. He struggled against the ropes to no avail.

He heard boots approaching, snapping twigs as they came near. He near pissed himself as the kid crouched down in front of him. "My name is Elias Kettle," he said. "That's important, you know. We victims all have names, faces. Personalities." He pulled out a photograph—graphic and terrible—of himself from ten years before. "I've been drugged for sex myself, as you can see. Maybe you're the one who sold the stuff that I got slipped." Bob protested earnestly against his gag. "Maybe not. Either way, in the spirit of ensuring sex tomorrow actually be as proverbially 'hearts and flowers' as it should be, let's just consider this next part a public service."

As Elias gave a sudden push, Bob found himself rolled into a pre-dug grave. He wasn't alone in the dirt and more "salesmen" like him would come later. They wouldn't be found and the communities that lost them wouldn't mourn for long. "Happy Valentine's Day," Elias mused, shoveling soil onto Bob's face. "No means *no.*"

Paper-lace Heart by Andra Dill

A piercing breeze rippled through Jocelyn's cornsilk hair. Triangular snips of red construction paper swirled around her sneakers. Watching the current spiral them up like tiny red butterflies, she shifted on the butt-numbingly cold concrete steps. She should go inside. Let go of this anger, the fear.

Her fingers ached from clenching the thick folds of paper. With a snick of the blades, another petite wedge of paper fluttered to the ground. It had to be perfect. A brilliant display of her own tattered heart. An offering to yet another foster Mother, so this one wouldn't let Jocelyn go.

Of Reindeer, Fauns and Trolls by Joshua E. Borgmann

Rudolph the Red-Nosed Reindeer, Rudy to his friends, had spent over a month of the off season chatting up a faun named Lilith on Magi-Tinder. It was a lot of work considering that all the reindeer girls were always chasing after him, but he just wasn't into reindeer. What he really craved was a human girl, but he knew that relationships between magical creatures and humans were banned. Most humans didn't even believe in him beyond some silly holiday songs and television specials. However, fauns were magical creatures, and they were just human enough to get his motor running.

He'd struck out with the first two dozen of his Magi-Tinder matches because they thought that his being four legged just wasn't cute, so he'd visited a pretty witch down in Samhain Hollow who had given him a potion that would allow him to walk on two legs and grow hands whenever he wanted. While the transformation was quite painful, as one would expect of morphing muscle and bone and tearing of hooves, it worked. A quick update of his profile and he'd matched with Lilith, a woodland faun who lived out beyond Hunter's Way on the other side of Mythra, a great woodland city.

Lilith's home was quite a journey for Rudy, but they bonded online, chatting literally for days on end, as magical creatures didn't need much sleep. They soon made plans to meet at a Starfauns in Mythra on Valentine's Day.

When the day came, Rudy did himself up in a red suit that he had stolen from Santa and bought a bouquet of dandelions from an exotic goods shop. After a quick stop in Valentine's Alley for a box of chocolates, he was on his way. The journey was long, but when he saw Lilith in a short crimson dress that revealed plenty of her gorgeous legs, he knew it was worth it. He couldn't stop staring at her all through their lattes. For her part, she gobbled up the dandelions and told Rudy that she just might be in love.

A few hours later, Lilith asked Rudy to escort her home. They took a Bubblecar to the edge of the forest but had to walk from there. Lilith warned Rudy not to make noises in Hunter's Way because trolls were known poachers. However, not being used to walking on two legs, he kept breaking twigs. Suddenly, there were two booms. Rudolph saw a massive hole rip through Lilith's chest right before his neck exploded.

A troll couple walked down to their catch. The male laughed and said, "Look Bomdrella, we got Rudolph the Red. He'll look great above the fireplace."

Bomdrella smiled as she said, "Oh Mekial, what a grand surprise. This is the best Valentine's Day ever."

From that day forward, Rudolph and Lilith spent every Valentine's Day together, their dead eyes staring down on the troll's frequent feasting and love making.

Love Letters by David Simms

Billy sat in the middle of his room, the soft yellow bulb dulling the medicated glaze in his eyes. It couldn't faze his grin, though, as he thought of her.

Cassie.

She wouldn't miss Valentine's Day. Couldn't.

The letters he'd written to her splayed out in front of him on the cold floor. Her replies concealed his.

"Leave me alone."

"Come back."

"Let me out."

"Just let me die in peace."

His tears had finally dried as he willed her to visit him in his cell. The scratches on the walls, marks of his dedication to making it right. She had been with him for so long, too long to keep hiding.

On the first day she greeted him, his day exploded with a thrill he hadn't felt in years, if ever. He welled up, charged with a sensation so intimate, he couldn't describe it. Nor did he need to. Mom and Dad had kept him home from school ever since the incident, the one where the others came out to play. Out of all his newfound friends, Cassie had been the only one to shine within his heart. She'd spoken to him for only a few minutes, yet her words snared him like a bear trap.

The light faded again, the electricity dimming in the state facility. He craned his stiff neck to the door without a knob for signs of another delivery. Nothing. Nobody stood at the small window a few feet above his scraggly hair that he had been grooming for days in the event she visited.

Nothing. No letter peeking from under the door, no knock or buzzing in of family or friends. Why would they? Neither Mom nor Dad bothered at Christmas, so why would anyone for the holiday meant for a love of a different kind?

With a shiver, he sensed a change in the electricity around him. Flesh tickled, goosebumps formed.

She had heard him.

"It's time to let me go," she said. Billy spun to the door, expecting to see her coiled brown curls falling across her shoulders. The words, a spike to the sternum, stole the wind from him. His fingers tore at his eyes when she didn't materialize behind the protected glass.

"Show yourself," he screamed to her. "Don't leave me to them."

Yet she did, and his skull began to tingle. His vision blurred and the whispers of strangers crept in through his periphery. All except her. When he focused in on her face, the blackness washed over him once again.

When reality gripped hold of him some time later, Billy opened his eyes to find new wounds, mostly scratches and abrasions. A sliver of red on the mirror before him. He could recall none of what transpired.

In front of him lay new letters. One was marked by a familiar handwriting. "Love always," it read. "Farewell."

Yet he knew she would always be near, just not close enough.

The Nightmare by Robert Chester Ferguson Jr

The rain, it beat down,
  On a cold, lonely night.
  And me too scared
  To turn on the light.
  The room, it was dark
  As I stood all alone.
  My heart throbbed
  A frightened tone.
  I screamed out for help,
  But no one stirred.
  I was all alone,
  Yet footsteps, I heard.
  Then came that sound
  From within the hall,
  An echoing voice;
  The Satan's call.
  I grabbed my knife;
  I shook with fright.
  I saw the figure
  Against the night.
  I stabbed the figure
  With the night as cover.

And she cried out for help
It was my lover!

Misguided Ritual by N.M. Brown

It's Valentine's Day, one of the saddest days of the year for me. See, I've been a widower for six years now.

I was married to a woman named Ava for fifteen blissful years. We didn't have much in the beginning, but we were happy. She always said she'd rather struggle with a man that she loved than to have luxury with a man she didn't. Ava was good to me that way.

Anyway, six years ago today she was taken from me. It was February 14th, I wasn't feeling well. She went to the natural food market to get me some tea. Ava always made tea when I was sick, pampering me lovingly. She was just down one of the aisles and whoosh, her life snuffed out like a candle. She just dropped dead right there in the spices section. Thirty-four years old, healthier than I was. Just like that...one aneurysmal subarachnoid hemorrhage later and she's gone forever.

Food has no taste, water quenches no thirst and sleep gives no rest, not without Ava. I've prayed to Heaven and Hell. After days of searching I finally find a ritual of sorts. I've nothing to lose right?

The items are collected, the ritual performed. I feel no different after, just exhausted in every way one's spirit can be. Trying not to get my hopes up, I head to bed. Halfway through the day, the door makes a squeak it opens. I descend the stairs. There's my beautiful Ava. She places a bag of groceries down on the counter and takes out a box of tea.

"Babe, what happened to the car? I drove it to the store. When I came out it was gone," she explains. "I had to call one of those Uber things. The guy had packs of Cheez-Its in his car. I got your tea by the way." She kisses my cheek and pauses before proceeding to flit about the house, cleaning and arranging like no years have passed at all. I hug her fiercely and we make love like we haven't in years, literally.

The clock hits 7:20 PM and Ava screams! Her bones contort and her eyes freeze over. She clutches her heart and drops off the bed, rigid by the time she hits the ground. I faint, wake up, and it's morning again. Ava is laying on her side smiling at me, with no recollection of the night before.

It's been almost one year since this started. We wake up every day together and one night each week I go to bed a widower. I'm losing my mind. How many times do I have to watch this? It'll always be the last thing I see before I go to sleep and the first thing I think about in the morning. What's worse, her eyes are starting to look the same alive as they do when she's dead.

Button Girl by Matthew Clarke

Trish Dawson isn't like the other girls at Wheaton Academy.

Paddy Patterson in particular takes great pleasure in reminding her of this fact. Every year, on Valentine's Day, he would make a big show of presenting tacky cards to all of the girls in their class. All except Trish.

She would tell herself she didn't care. That he was ugly anyway. A bully.

It would be nice to get a card from *somebody* though.

Somebody other than her mother. Just once.

The other girls would follow her in the playground, sniggering, calling her names, making no effort whatsoever to be discreet. *Button Bitch. Stitch Face. Plastic Princess.*

Sometimes, she would laugh along with them in a futile attempt to dull the pain. Most of the time though, she would spend her lunch break in the toilets, weeping strands of fine black thread and hating herself. Perhaps one day she would have enough thread to make that noose. Turn disability in to productivity.

Today was February 10th. Four days until the big day. Perhaps she would make herself throw up in the morning so she could stay at home, spend another exciting day in front of her mirror, staring at her stupid, sewn-on eyes and cursing God for making her this way.

But then, something incredible happened. There was a new boy, from out of town—the most beautiful thing she'd ever laid her little black disks on. From the blonde curls that kissed his forehead with each step, to the gleaming, silver zipper that formed his mouth.

He met her eyes. Caught her staring. The open zipper caught the playful sunlight of that chilly, February morning as it pulled into a smile. The pull tab in the corner jostled cheekily.

He said his name was Samuel. Samuel Hurst.

She told him hers. Several of the other kids in the playground had formed a crowd around them, gawking, but Trish didn't care.

She had a feeling that this year, she would be getting that card.

Fireworks by Dawn DeBraal

Robert was going to ask Anita for her hand in marriage. He had everything planned, the ring, dinner, champagne, and roses in an outdoor pavilion on Valentine's Day. He would ask, and when she said yes, a complete choreographed firework display as they kissed, sealing the deal. It was perfect.

He had set everything up before Anita got there. Dinner went well. Robert walked Anita outside. There sat the champagne and a dozen roses. He looked into her eyes as he got down on one knee.

"Yes!" Anita shouted. Robert hit the remote. Fireworks shot the stars out of Anita's eyes.

Not Quite Tailor-Made by DJ Elton

Landy was a clever and perfectly organized witch. On Mondays she would do her visual work, thinking of a man she wanted to engage and have call on her. She chose his hair colour, eyes and attributes of a pleasantly handsome face. She paid special attention to his body, its strength, muscle and skin texture, as well as his state of mind. He needed to be intelligent, capable, not overconfident or arrogant. Good mannered and able to make her laugh. All these traits would complement the perfect Valentine. And he had to be emotionally available. After all, she was a credible witch, deserving of good company.

On Wednesdays she would set the herbs, creating a tincture, lotion, or sometimes a small doll. Her crow Bal helped source the raw materials, and would deliver the goods to the right house, workplace or street at the estimated time the man would be there. Practise makes perfect. Each year she had accumulated a wonderful collection of men, none of whom had an inkling about each others' existence, for Landy was most discreet. And after a weekend of her company, the man of the week would not remember a thing. This worked well for quite some time.

Unfortunately, the law of cause and effect is such that nothing can remain static, even in the work of witching. This time, things had gone terribly wrong. There was a huge glitch in Landy's karma. The man who arrived at Landy's country home on the Friday night was not alone, as they always were. He had three others with him, all similar. Other than that, he was not of Landy's design. This one was rough, obese, foul-smelling and swore constantly. Landy was unimpressed, but there was not much she could do about it. She continued to play her part in the game although it became more and more confusing. He was the exact opposite of what she had pre-arranged and this became apparent by the end of the weekend.

Nothing went according to her plan.

They found her three weeks later; her magic had been unable to save her body.

Bal the crow had died in grief.

The Sign by Dawn DeBraal

The candles flickered softly. Their Valentine's dinner ended when Darrell told Brenda that he loved her but had some doubts. Darrell said he needed a sign, a big one, to help him make his decision. Brenda pulled away, hurt. She thought they were getting engaged and instead realized Darrell had doubts. Brenda folded her napkin, placing it next to her plate.

"Do you want a sign, Darrell? I'll give you a sign to help you decide." Brenda stood up, snatching her hand from Darrell's hand, walking straight out the door. Darrell wished she would have turned right; that was his sign.

Just Dessert by Sheila Shedd

We'd met three months before, an all night thing at a club called *Sprechen*. Purple strobes and long-winded jams featuring a French horn backed by a theremin had me tired of the scene. I took a comfortable, isolated seat upstairs overlooking the rave, and Keven sat beside me. With the nighttime attractiveness of longish hair and an open wallet, I allowed him my company.

We chatted amiably for three hours; I was forward and charming at first, but as the mesmerizing effects of four Zombies wore thin, I found him self-obsessed and maudlin, talking at length about tactics of survival, or perhaps an escape…a contingency for some worst case scenario he had no reason to believe would ever materialize. When he finally drew breath, I made my exit, giving him a standard-issue cheek kissing. Sometime during the evening I must have also given over my number, and with that, some shred of hope for a future engagement.

I received his fifth invitation in February, a text asking me to dinner. Would I please join him in the city this Friday night? He was having friends, he said, for pasta and, to my delight, his special Tiramisu, made the traditional way, ladyfinger cookies layered in cream and soaked in Borghetti liqueur. This, he somehow knew or perhaps just guessed, was my favorite dessert—a true weakness of mine.

I didn't think his persistence strange; I gathered from our single evening that he was obsessed and juvenile. That he was a paranoid lunatic wasn't out of the question. But, alone on the nightshift, I had very few friends, and I would be alone, again, on Valentine's Day.

I arrived a bit late; fashionably, I suppose. Dinner had been served to three quiet guests who appeared more interested in their wine than the barely-sauced angel hair. They turned as I entered and I detected a blush of guilt, as though I'd walked in on children doing something they knew they oughtn't. Keven rounded the table and brought me into the fold; his hand was warm and it gripped more intimately than I was comfortable with. Still, I walked gracefully forward and took the seat that had been reserved for me.

More wine was poured, and, after two glasses, the company relaxed. Keven was polite and attentive, but the real conversation and laughter always circled back to memories and anecdotes between old friends, the type that serve to make one feel forever an outsider.

Not a moment too soon, our host went into the kitchen and returned with the famous dessert; my mouth watered in anticipation as the dish was set upon the table.

"Oh God!" I screamed when the cake was revealed. "What…what is this?!"

"Your favorite, my dear," Keven whispered.

"But…oh, God…the blood…"

"From the lady fingers, sweetheart. Happy Valentine's Day."

"It's…so much blood," I cried, looking at the dismembered digits. "It'll spoil the cream!"

Keven frowned.

We were married that spring.

Jane's Heartless Ex by N.M. Brown

It's my first Valentine's Day with my new boyfriend Derek. He had a rough break up around Christmas. It was public knowledge that his ex Jane was crazy. It's a wonder they lasted as long as they did. But anyway, it's a day of love, so I'm bringing him dinner to make the holiday extra special.

He texted me earlier in the day to let me know the door was unlocked so I let myself inside. His apartment's dark; the smell of copper assaults my senses.

I find him laying in a puddle of blood on the floor. His skin is cold and his eyes are frozen open, lifeless. There's a bloodied note pinned to his skin next to a gaping hole in his chest.

You stole Derek's heart from me, so I thought I'd take it back.

Love-Jane

Unrequited Love by N.M. Brown

My girl Mary and I have been chatting online for almost eight months now. I still have the Christmas card she sent me. I read the message written inside of it every day.

Merry Christmas Bobby! I wish I was with you! Love - Mary

There was a red and green address label attached to the upper left corner of the envelope, so I decided to fly out to surprise her for Valentine's Day.

Sweat covered my palms as I stood at her door, almost causing the flowers I brought to slip from my hands. She'd be so shocked to see me.

A man greeted me from the other side, surprised to see a stranger bearing gifts. I wasn't worried about him though; he went down easy once the blade slipped into his heart.

Mary came running into the room upon hearing the *thud* of his body hitting the floor. She stopped cold as our eyes met and a dreadful recognition washed over her face.

Bert...no, not again! I have a restraining order! How did you find me?!?

A frenzied glint creeps into my eyes as I present her with the Christmas card she sent "Bobby."

"There are so many variations for the name Robert. It's one of the more versatile ones, isn't it?" I mused as tears slid down her face.

"Happy Valentine's Day, Mary."

I Heart Art by Matthew Clarke

Tonight.

Fourteen years of sacrifice have led me to this moment in time. I've risked jobs, relationships, and family. But compared to this, nothing else matters.

I have spent the last twelve months carefully selecting and watching lucky number fourteen. I know Rosaline's schedule, passwords, favourite foods. Predictable. Delectable.

She will leave Tucker's Hardware at six-thirty precisely, remove her red headphones (*I have already decided that I will be keeping those*) from her satchel, continue down Edmund Street, and take a left down the alleyway that runs between the bookstore and the printer shop.

My vehicle is already parked at the other end of the alley. I know she will see it and pause, for I have been parking it by her workplace, and outside her house, for the last two days. Her hesitation will be her downfall.

She doesn't even scream. They normally do when they wake up, bound to a metal slab in a nondescript basement. I guess I underestimated her. I pretend it doesn't bother me, but behind my friendly smile I am an obelisk of rage. I step aside and show her my collection, the jars on my bookshelf, each carefully labelled with a year and a name. The last in the row bears her name and today's date: February 14 – 2020. That's when the screaming begins. I try to calm her, tell her how lucky she is to become the crowning piece of my artwork, but she just won't listen. With a sigh, I quickly open her chest cavity and remove her heart with surgical precision—a far cry from my first Valentine. What a mess that was. I hold the organ out for us both to admire. She doesn't say anything, although her mouth is trying to form words and her eyelids are fluttering. I think she is giving her approval. As the beating slows, I give it a tender kiss and carefully ease it into her jar. The butterflies come as the formaldehyde takes on a slight pink tinge.

Now, by this point you might be thinking I'm insane, sadistic, unhinged. But there are many people out there who would disagree with you.

I pull out my iPhone and take several pictures of the finished piece before uploading them to my online portfolio. The bidding for my Valentine's collection immediately skyrockets. I slip on Rosaline's headphones, plug them into my phone jack and listen to the frantic pinging of the bids. My latest piece quickly surpasses my Christmas collection by several million.

Assurances by Chris Bannor

She stared into the deep wells of his soul and brought her fingers up to gently caress his face. Her nails scratched softly across his skin, making a scratching sound against his stubble. He was like every other man she'd loved.

Beautiful.

Intelligent.

Independent.

Successful.

His eyes gazed at her with absolute affection and there was nothing more he wanted than to please her. He breathed her every wish like a command to his soul. She'd made sure of it with the spell.

Because she would not allow this one to be like every other man in her life.

Unfaithful.

Letter to Juliet by Wendy Cheairs

Dearest Juliet,

The chance to write someone in literature is too hard to resist this romantic season. My heart is full of love but alas, there is no one that I am attached to. Instead, I write a letter of appreciation to the famous historical ladies of the written word that I wish to woo, win over for the love of ages. I need that love, I need that forever love that everyone shall speak of evermore. What do I do? I know there is no reply, for you exist in the mind of all those who have read Shakespeare but this letter travels deep into Verona to wait for someone to read, sigh and continue to see all the messages that still come to your forever existence in the world. The love that shall not die; it is a tomb with you and the beloved Romeo of old. Which I too need, someone that loves me as much as Romeo dared love you. What do I do? How do I find her? Someone like you, my Juliet?

With an open heart,

Beloved in New Jersey

A letter returned days later from Italy; I ripped it open. Some Italian woman wrote me back, taken with my words.

New Jersey,

To find the love of ages one must be open and truthful. Follow the steps laid out for you in literature, and you too shall find love.

Modern Juliet

She attached a recipe for a love potion, I quickly made the sweet recipe that tasted of cherries and wine over my lips. As my last breath began to fade into the world, her spirit appeared, laughing. Then I understood, I saw, it was not real, it was just a story and mine was forgotten.

Together Forever by Josh R. Hunt

Between them lay a wedding ring, a diary and a happy couple smiling from a photograph. Madam Za arranged the items into a triangle, and gestured to each one in turn.

"The three anchors," she said. "Emotion. Possession. Identification. These ensure that the spirit we summon to our world is the one we call for, and no other. Now we need a beacon to light their way."

Professor Crowther opened the case by his side and extracted an intricate device, a cube of shining metal with dials and notches on every surface.

"This was the project I was working on when my wife chose to…leave this world," said Crowther. "She had always said I was too focussed on my research. I would stay up for days at a time trying to perfect it. I missed birthdays. Anniversaries. Funerals. Now she's gone, and without her my work is meaningless."

Madam Za nodded.

"This item is charged with regret and desire," she said. "It represents the divide that tore you and your wife apart, and now it will be the light that guides her back to us. Place it in the centre of the triangle, and prepare yourself."

With trembling hands, Crowther followed Madam Za's instructions. As soon as the device touched the table's surface, Madam Za began to chant. The frail lilt that Crowther recognised soon grew and deepened. It boomed out of the ancient woman's throat, filled the room, shook his bones. His wedding ring glowed with a piercing blue. His wife's diary followed, then their photograph, then his metal box, all lit as if consumed by fire.

The air flickered as a slender body rose above their heads. Pale, transparent, but somehow more real than anything Crowther had ever seen. The body stretched, flexing its limbs as if for the first time.

Then she turned to face him.

"Darling…" said his wife, her voice a distant echo, a sultry whisper, a vocalisation of his every memory of her. She was perfect. She was beautiful.

She was here.

Her spirit lowered a gentle hand, open in forgiveness. Crowther extended his own, reaching across the table.

He grasped his device and flicked a switch.

Blinding light tore through the room. Madam Za reeled, her ritual chant dying in her throat, while above them both, Crowther's wife screamed. Her shining body writhed and squirmed, stabbed by the light of the box as though it were daggers. Her glowing limbs twisted in on themselves, each fold slow and torturous. With a final, desperate cry, her soul vanished into the metal box. Crowther slammed another switch and extinguished the light.

As Madam Za staggered to her feet, Crowther clutched the device to his chest in a lover's embrace.

"Thank you," he breathed. "I couldn't have finished my research without you."

Madam Za shook her head, face drained of colour.

"This is monstrous," she said. "I want no part of this".

Crowther scowled at her.

"I wasn't talking to you," he said.

Gomorrah by Daileas Duclo

This was the one place on the Strip where you could truly get whatever you wanted. More than anything, Monica really hoped that was true. She had a very traumatic childhood; suffice it to say she was her daddy's favorite.

Her mother died when she was sixteen and she ran away from Tucson with no intention of ever going back because daddy gave her way too much attention. She tried counseling, tried taking her problem to the police, and she even tried drugs; none of those things panned out. The Family said they could help you fix anything for a price. She agreed to their terms without question. After all, working for them was a small price to pay for peace of mind. Now she finally got her own red room, and this time she was the one who had come home early. This time she had the big stick, and by god, he was going to endure it.

As she stood over the prone figure, whose hands were bound and tendons severed, she couldn't help but laugh.

"Daddy, don't you want to play with your little girl?" she taunted him as she ran the straight razor gently across his bare chest and face. She stroked him with the blade and shushed him, placing her finger at his lips before settling the blade near his groin.

"I know you probably forgot today was my birthday, but my new family didn't. They said I could have whatever I wanted, and I told them I wanted this!" she exclaimed before wrenching the blade upward and severing the trembling man's member. As the blood sprayed out across the room and upon her frilly dress, which was fitted for a girl much younger than she was, Monica couldn't help but feel like this was home.

Gomorrah was her place and she certainly felt satisfied.

Valentines Surprise by Amber M. Simpson

Carly followed the trail of rose petals into the house, giddy with excitement. She'd been sure Blake wouldn't take their first Valentine's Day together seriously—opposed as he was to all commercialized holidays—but apparently, she'd been wrong.

The petals led her upstairs to the unlit bedroom, his form a dark lump in bed. With a girlish squeal, she leaped in beside him and nuzzled his broad, warm chest—so hairy…so sticky…and so not Blake's.

Jerking away, Carly switched on the bedside lamp and screamed in shock and horror. The knife in the stranger's hand gleamed as bright as his eyes beneath the bloody homemade mask of Blake's face.

Time Wounds All Heals by Scott Deegan

Our time together ended long ago, and there's no way to regain what was lost. So why is she creeping back into my mind and my life? Little things that bring her back, a song, the way the light falls through the window, and of course the news reports. The story is still big news around here, her disappearance and no answers. People still look at me like I did something to her. I didn't, I never could.

Beth and I thought we were happy. We convinced others we were. But Beth had a sadness to her; deep down inside where I was never allowed, she was hurting. She never talked about it but I could see it in her eyes, that pain she internalized. I didn't know the story behind those eyes, not until they started the investigation.

It was from the first news reports and then the detectives that I learned about the death of her parents. The murder-suicide that happened after she was sent to spend the summer with her grandparents on their farm. How before they died they erased all traces of Beth from their lives cleaned out her room, made it into an office, and burnt everything that proved she had ever been a part of their family. How that must have hurt the twelve-year-old girl, knowing your parents didn't want you so much that they erased you and then ended their lives to be rid of you. It was thirteen years after the tragedy that Beth disappeared, on the anniversary of her parents death. I didn't do it. I didn't even know that she disappeared until days later.

It was the night she came back from visiting her grandparents that she started acting strange and trying to pick a fight. I couldn't do anything right, I was breathing wrong, I only said the wrong things, and when she tried to stab me I left. I went to my brother's house and stayed there. The detective believes that sometime during those five days the incident occurred. I came back to find the house we shared ransacked, and of all things hoof prints burned into both the carpeting and hardwood floors. The investigation led nowhere and the police focused on me, as did most of the community. I should have left town the way I was looked at and treated by my neighbors, but I didn't do anything, and this is my home.

The only evidence that was found at the scene was a contract in some ancient language signed by what I later learned were her parents and stuck to the door with a goat's horn. Her grandmother would only cross herself and say a prayer when asked about it; her grandfather would just stare at you. I still don't know what happened.

Now, 13 years later, someone is leaving notes signed with her name on my door. Oh, and the hoof prints that surround the house every morning.

My Crazy Ex by Nerisha Kemraj

She looked at me with crazy eyes then turned the blade on me.
   "If I can't have you, no one will," she laughed with insane glee.
   I sat there bound and gagged, there was nothing I could do,
   Then I spotted my girl, Mary-Beth, we had to make it through.
   Jane screamed for my attention then,
   "It's Valentine's Day, my angel, Kyle, thank you for the gift."
   She turned towards Mary-Beth,
   then thrust the knife, so swift!
   A scream of rage escaped me as my love fell to the floor.
   "Damn you, Jane!" I shouted, as Mary-Beth was no more.

Repurposed for the Modern Audience by Wendy Cheairs

"How do you keep any power in this day in age where gods are just myths and legends?" the ghostly figure asked, barely tangible, lost in the echoes of time to the youthful man drinking yet another glass of deep red wine.

"Simple, my dear forgotten one. My holiday was taken by the Christians, made into a holiday that became popular. Now I survive through the year, my name as a myth, but the power they give me each ides of February feed me through the year."

"Valentine's Day, bah. That has nothing to do with you."

"But it does. It was my holiday, fertility and lust, and what is it now about? Chocolate, sex, champagne and lust, cover in reds and pinks, dusted with greed and Americanized to the point of being forgotten, brings the hostile edge into relationships, everything that I am, just different packaging. Maybe you should try it and not just fade off into lost tombs."

"It shouldn't work?"

"Ask Ostara. She is living off Easter, which they also took from her and repackaged. She is alive and well somewhere in Germany, enjoying her life."

"But you are a faun. How is that romantic?"

"I am Faunus the faun, and who said I was romantic? It is about lust, my boy, and I am the embodiment of lust redone for the modern era." The youth spoke with a wicked smile, showing some of the teeth no one naturally had.

Playtime by James Pyles

"You told me you loved me."

Wayne Moreno was in a cell in a secure wing of County Jail on suicide watch. However, the guards couldn't have been prepared for the impossible.

"Wake up."

Moreno's eyes fluttered. His cell was only dimly illuminated, but it was as if the little girl shone in her own strange light.

"Dreaming. Yeah…"

"You're not dreaming, Wayne."

This time she was demanding. He opened his eyes and she was still there. Wayne sat up on his bed. "What the screw?"

The girl couldn't have been more than seven or eight. A white girl, but really white, with no skin colour at all. It was the same with her hair. Her eyes were dead black, like a doll's eyes.

"My name is Susie. Remember me? I've come to visit you."

"How you know my name?"

"I know all about you. I know you like to hurt little girls."

"You get out. Guard! Where the hell are the guards?"

"You're not a nice man and you say dirty words."

"Get the out of here or I'll do more than say dirty words." He was angry and confused and she really pissed him off with what she said about him.

"Really, Wayne? I'm not scared of you. I'm not scared of anyone."

"Who cares? Guard!"

"No one can hear you. My friends made sure they're all asleep. When they wake up, they won't remember anything."

Then she grinned and he saw her fangs for the first time.

"We have all night long to play, Wayne."

"You stay away!" He had climbed back onto his bed and pressed himself against the cinder block wall.

Susie placed an alabaster hand on the door of his cell and it swung open effortlessly. "I heard that you liked playing with children."

She took a step into the cell.

"You come anywhere near me and I'll kill you."

"You can't kill me, Wayne. I'm already dead." She took a second step in and then stopped.

"But if you don't like me, I brought some friends. Maybe you'll like one of them."

Out of the shadows behind her, shapes began to move. Then one by one they appeared in the pale light. There were more children like Susie, boys and girls all with unnaturally light skin, dark eyes, and red lips. Some smiled, some leered. One little girl crouched down and hissed like a feral cat, baring gleaming fangs.

"Who would you like to play with first?"

"Please don't hurt me." He was sobbing now, his body shaking with terror. He still couldn't look away. What would they do to him if he couldn't see them coming?

They lunged at him all at once.

The children had all died terrible, agonizing, and unjust deaths; when he tortured them it lasted for hours. The only thing Susie and her friends could do was make sure Wayne's soul got a good taste of Hell before he actually made the trip.

Wrong Person, Right Place by N.M. Brown

I miss my husband. It's our fifteenth Valentine's Day as a couple and he has to work. They say that one of the keys to a great marriage is compromise, so I'm taking it upon myself to improvise. We've sent messages back and forth all day, along with some very private pictures. He gets off in one hour; that gives me just enough time to prepare for his homecoming.

I went out and bought two gorgeous ribeyes at the market with some asparagus and hollandaise (his favorite). There's a bottle of wine chilling in the fridge and my YouTube account is all set up with a romantic, sexy-time playlist. My mind reels with adoration when I think of how long we've been together.

On the table are freshly chilled chocolate covered strawberries, two wine glasses, a clean ashtray, joint and lighter. The steaks are resting and warmed along with the veggies. The dining room is set for the perfect evening.

Onto the bedroom; I've placed flameless candles around the room. Hubby hates a hot room, and our bed is made with fresh silken sheets.

Now to get myself ready! I place my clothes on the bed; he likes me in pinks best. I scent them with his favorite perfume. My blood warms at the thought of his touch.

Atop the counter sits a lovingly written note that reads, *Your Valentine is waiting in the bath. Help yourself to the table, then come on in. I love you.*

My body is relieved of the weight of my clothes as I start to run the bath. The scented body wash is poured in. I watch the still water start to pop and bubble with excitement. Slowly, I lower myself into the bath, letting the warmth of the water envelop me like a blanket. I start playing music on my phone as I lay my head back and close my eyes. The front door knob squeaks as it opens, then I hear it close; hubby's home!!!

From the living room, I hear the sound of shoes shuffling to the dining room table. I wriggle my frame down further into the water, smiling wickedly. The flick of the lighter sounds and soon I can smell the sweet scent of burned rope. A *POP* resounds as a wine cork dislodges from its bottle. I wonder if he's gotten my note yet.

Then a crashing sound startles me, like something being knocked over. I can hear footsteps walking closer to the bathroom. My joy is like a child's on Christmas! "Baby! You alright out there? I cleaned all day to make everything nice, you gonna share that? I'm waaaaiiittttttiiiinnng," I sing out to him.

There's no response, but the bathroom doorknob turns. Suddenly the music is interrupted by a text message alert. It's from my husband.

Hey Honey. I'm sorry I'm stuck at the office for a little bit longer. I love you. Can't wait to see you

Getting Handsy by Jason Myers

The advertisement said "Win a new Ford in February." The fine folks at Palmer Ford were nice enough to donate a brand new F150 with a two-year lease to the winner. The radio station, 100.5 The Buzz, was hosting, giving hourly updates to its precious listeners. The contest seemed simple enough; the person who kept their hand on the truck the longest wins. The contestants were chosen by winning random call-in contests and the whole thing was to take place on Valentine's Day weekend.

Roughly five hours in and the participants had dropped from the original eighteen down to eleven. The radio jockeys were doing their best to ridicule the players as well as keep the folks listening at home aware of the winter blast arriving sometime later today. Temperatures were dropping almost as fast as the contestants who were unwilling to keep their bare hands on the cold aluminum of the tailgate.

"Ladies and gentlemen, The Buzz is pleased to announce another seven contestants have left us to drive home in their old cars here in the last hour, refusing to keep a hand on the Ford in the frigid cold. We are down to our final four."

From four to two in the matter of an hour and a half. Temperatures now dipped to the single digits. One man and one woman remained. Both on opposite sides of the blue pickup. It had been an ongoing power struggle for more than half a day and no one imagined the contest would still be taking place. The jockeys had long since packed it in and were only getting updates via text messages from onlookers and passersby.

With the morning cold and wind gusting madly the ending was in sight.

The radio station rushed back to the dealership just as the male patron on the right side of the half ton finally gave in to what can only be assumed to be hypothermia. He lasted a total of thirteen hours and forty-seven minutes. The new crew for The Buzz were queueing up the mics to announce the winner of the Brand New Ford and get in whatever quick interview she was willing to give. "Photo opportunity to show her finally breaking away from the half ton truck, then it's all yours."

As the local news crews began rolling live, the disc jockeys began their planned winner's speech. At the moment they announced her win, the excitement causing heart palpitations, her body, already in shock, immediately went into cardiac arrest.

She died on the scene, live and local, next to her brand new powder blue half ton.

Lesson For The Beast by Galina Trefil

As the checker scanned each individual item just a little too slowly, her thick false eyelashes batted at the customer. She leaned forward, pushing her upper arms into the sides of her cleavage to maximize their prominence. Her bright cherry lips curved upwards into a scintillating smile. "Hey, sweetheart, how's your evening going?" she purred in a decidedly bedroom voice.

Standing a few feet away from them, beside her own grocery cart, seventy-five-year-old Coral stiffened. She eyed the young man's purchases—specifically, the heart-shaped box of chocolates, the flowers, and, to top it all off, baby diapers. How much more obviously in a relationship could he be? Coral glared as the checker twisted to showcase her décolletage even more.

Would he take the bait and flirt back? No. He only shrugged in response to the checker's question. She made a few more attempts to engage him, but he remained evasive until he finally left.

Coral pushed her cart forward, scowling. She knew this type of beautiful, clever monster all too well. They got a high out of inserting themselves into and damaging the love lives of other people. And, to a homewrecker, there was no day more important than the holiday that was swiftly approaching. During the celebration of romantic love, this beast thrived off the knowledge that husbands might be fantasizing about her seductiveness, rather than their own wives. But, more than that, it fed off the fact that wives and girlfriends knew their husbands were doing this. It was a game of power, masquerading under the guise of sexuality. To the beast the episode was a mere diversion, but to those who felt jilted, there were severe relationship consequences.

After paying for her own things, Coral sighed, "Oh, dear, you really must be careful. One of these days you might stomp on the wrong wife's toes."

"Excuse me?" Yes, of course the beast looked offended, pretending that she didn't know exactly what Coral meant.

"There was this lady back in the day that went after my husband. She didn't really want him; just wanted me to be miserable and alone. So do you know what I did, dear?"

"Ma'am, I'm not really interested in hearing your life story. You need to move along so that other customers—"

"I snuck into her house and put bleach in her shampoo bottle. Blinded her for life and she was never even able to prove who did it." Coral chuckled soullessly. "I doubt that she tried to break up other peoples' marriages after that again...."

The checker paled and gaped.

"Most wives won't go to that extreme, I know. But every once in a while, dear, you might meet a wicked, crazy bitch who won't take kindly to her territory being intruded upon." Coral started to leave, but then turned back. "Oh, and, dear, the batteries are on aisle twelve. A date with them may not be ideal, but at least it won't be dangerous. Happy Valentine's Day. Please, be smarter."

Crazy Daisy by Matthew A. Clarke

He loves me. He loves me not.

Daisy had been obsessing over Kieran since she first saw him at the drive in. He was sat with a blonde in the front of his Cadillac, laughing and eating popcorn as the giants on screen ran from a masked killer. That was a lifetime ago.

He loves me.

Daisy paced the room, wiping sweat from her brow with her free hand. She was running out of space, unsure she could fit another incision on her canvas. Kieran kicked and screamed as she drew the blade across his neck.

He loves me not.

Papercuts by Natasha Sinclair

Red is my favourite colour. Especially when I dream of it painted on those fat-cats relentlessly chasing the green.

The automatic dialer pings, the next one squawks like a fork scraping a plate, piercing my ear. A flesh and bone robot vacant, I wait in my place with words that sound like they come from a smile, as automatic as the damned dialler—damned like me. The rest of them, they chat in between, mindless as their words. "You doing anything special for Valentine's?" All on the monotonous automatic cycle. Fuck, one day my eyes will get stuck facing the inside my skull from rolling so hard. Every day is exactly the same, spin the record one more time, minions of the green dream. Being spoon-fed their milestones and conversation from those ghouls rolling in it. Never any paper cuts though, it's all digital now, as fake as the happiness and life it professes to give.

Martha passes her heart-shaped chocolates around the desks. Team gorging camaraderie.

Time to redecorate this beige hell box, get down with the season. I reach into my bag, pull out the pistol, and set loose. "Happy Valentine's Day."

Thanks For Reading!

Thank you for reading our macabre collection!

Please don't forget to leave a review and check out our contributing author's Amazon pages for more of their epic words!

Cassandra Angler, Angela Glover, M. Ennenbach, P.J. Blakey-Novis, Sea Caummisar, Galina Trefil, DJ Elton, N.M. Brown, Scott Deegan, Alanna Robertson-Webb, Terry Miller, Trisha McKee, Dawn DeBraal, Archit Joshi, Galina Trefil, Andrew Kurtz, Jason Myers, Andra Dill, Matthew A. Clarke, Alexander Shedd, Sheila Shedd, Ximena Escobar, Nerisha Kemraj, Zoey Xolton, Kevin J. Kennedy, Chris Miller, Lea Vida Del Moro, Wendy Cheairs, Amber M. Simpson, James Pyles, Robert Chester Ferguson Jr, Danielle Sandidge, Joel R. Hunt, Lance Dale, Nicole Henning, Nico Bell, Joshua E. Borgmann, Natasha Sinclair, Daileas Duclo, David Simms, Andrea Allison, Chris Bannor, Aaron Channel, Tina Merry, Aindrila Roy and Zachary C. Collier

Printed in Poland
by Amazon Fulfillment
Poland Sp. z o.o., Wrocław

54914848R00106